CW01082459

THE SALEM BELLE

THE

SALEM BELLE

A TALE OF 1692

Ebenezer Wheelwright,

edited, with an introduction and notes,
by Richard Kopley

THE PENNSYLVANIA STATE UNIVERSITY PRESS

University Park, Pennsylvania

Library of Congress Cataloging-in-Publication Data
Wheelwright, Ebenezer, 1800–1877, author.
The Salem belle : a tale of 1692 / Ebenezer Wheelwright ;
edited with an introduction and notes by
Richard Kopley.
pages   cm
Summary: "A historical novel, first published in 1842,
about vengeance mistaken for religious fervor, set
against the Salem witchcraft trials of 1692. This novel was
a critical source for Nathaniel Hawthorne's The Scarlet Letter.
Introduced and annotated by Hawthorne scholar
Richard Kopley"—Provided by publisher.
Includes bibliographical references.
ISBN 978-0-271-07116-9 (cloth : alk. paper)
1. Trials (Witchcraft)—Fiction
2. Revenge—Fiction.
3. Salem (Mass.)—History—Colonial period, ca.
1600–1775—Fiction.
I. Kopley, Richard, editor. II. Title.
PS3167.W28S35 2016
813'.3—dc23
2015032537

for

Nina Baym

CONTENTS

———————

ACKNOWLEDGMENTS

———————

I am very grateful to Patrick Alexander, director of Penn State Press, and Kendra Boileau, editor in chief of Penn State Press, for their strong support of this book. I am grateful, too, to the Press's editorial board and to the book's outside readers. I am thankful to Jennifer Norton, associate press director and design and production manager; Laura Reed-Morrison, managing editor; Julie Schoelles, manuscript editor; Hannah Hebert, editorial assistant; and Susan Silver, copyeditor. And I am also thankful to my excellent research intern, Samantha Gilmore, and the wonderful intern coordinator for the Department of English at Penn State, University Park, Liz Jenkins. I am glad to recognize the important support of Madlyn Hanes, vice president of the Commonwealth Campuses at Penn State; and Melanie Hatch, chancellor and chief academic officer at Penn State, DuBois.

It has been a pleasure to exchange e-mails with others working on the Wheelwright family, Jack Santos and Brandon Schrand, as well as with Edward G. Lengel. I have enjoyed my research at the Congregational Library in Boston and the assistance of Margaret Bendroth, executive director, and her staff. The staff at the Microtext Department of the Boston Public Library has also been very helpful. And, as always, I am indebted to the fine staff of the Pattee Library and Paterno Library at Penn State.

I am appreciative of the permissions that have been granted for manuscript passages in this book. Thanks go to the Baker Library Historical Collections, the Huntington Library, the Kent State University Libraries, the Lilly Library, the Massachusetts Historical Society, and the Phillips Library of the Peabody Essex Museum.

I am happy to acknowledge Eric Holzenberg and Arthur L. Schwartz, curators of the exhibition The Grolier Club Collects II, which included the 1880 volume *Worth Keeping*, featuring a piece by Ebenezer Wheelwright. The event was ably facilitated by Grolier Club exhibitions manager Jennifer K. Sheehan.

I am thankful to members of the Nathaniel Hawthorne Society for their warm collegiality and scholarly interest.

And, finally, I am thankful to my wife, Amy Golahny; our children, Emily and Gabe; my mother, Irene Kopley; and my father-in-law, Yuda Golahny—they have encouraged me in my work and welcomed Ebenezer as a long-lost uncle.

NOTE ON THE TEXT

———————

The text offered here is that of the first edition, the 1842 *The Salem Belle: A Tale of 1692*. Misspellings and errors in punctuation have been silently corrected. I have modernized the text as little as possible.

INTRODUCTION
Richard Kopley

Commenting on what the family had had for dinner—"a piece of
beef 'with a streak of fat & a streak of lean'"—Isaac G. Reed, of
Waldoboro, Maine, wrote on January 26, 1843, to his daughter
Mary, then in Boston, "It might well have pleased Jack Spratt
& his wife, tho I think they could not have 'licked the platter
clean,' unless they were of the dimensions of the sons of Anak,
or had the voracity, which Lyford & Henry must have had when
they arrived at Worcester after having 'put up' eight days in
'the shed,' with blankets enough for themselves & horse & to
make a curtain besides."[1] Reed easily relied here on a nursery rhyme, still familiar today, "Jack Sprat," and on a biblical
phrase perhaps less familiar today, but accessible, "the sons of
Anak," the giants who were found by Moses's spies in the land
of Canaan.[2] But utterly unfamiliar today is Reed's reference to
"Lyford & Henry" in Worcester, Massachusetts, after eight days
in the shed. Who were Lyford and Henry? What shed? Reed's
source, as he soon acknowledged, was the 1842 novel *The Salem
Belle*, a tale of love, vengeance, and guilt, set against the Salem

witchcraft delusion of 1692. It is an engaging work whose recovery today is warranted on its own merits—and then additionally for its critical importance in Nathaniel Hawthorne's masterpiece, *The Scarlet Letter*.

Reed continued, "So far & a little farther, I have read in 'The Salem Belle.' I have gotten to the time when Trellison procures the name of the belle to be added to the list of the proscribed, & I think [the] book, so far, well written—especially the sermons of Willard & of Mather. I have read without an effort to discover 'inconsistencies,' and therefore have found but few. And I am too little versed in the niceties of history to detect anachronisms or other errors."[3] Mary's father had read more than half of the book. He had encountered, among other incidents, James Lyford and young Henry taking refuge during a snowstorm in a shed outside of Worcester as they journeyed by sleigh from Hadley, Massachusetts, to Boston, and he had come upon the two dramatic sermons at the center of the novel (*Salem Belle*, 110–11, 113–17)[4] and the subsequent accusation of witchcraft by Trellison, the rejected suitor, against the beautiful young woman who had turned him down, Mary Graham—James Lyford's sister—"the Salem belle" (125).

Perhaps Reed had his daughter Jane Ann's copy of the novel, in which she had written "By Mr. Wheelwright."[5] An earlier letter to Jane Ann's sister Mary from a friend, Sarah R. Derby, asked, "Have you seen Mr. and Mrs. Wheelwright lately? Have they moved from Dover Street? Please give my love to them."[6] A quick check of Boston directories reveals that the "Mr. Wheelwright" who had moved from Dover Street was Ebenezer Wheelwright. And he had moved to 3 Temple Place, the address of Charles Tappan, of the firm Tappan and Dennet, the

publishers of *The Salem Belle*.[7] Indeed, the author had inscribed
a copy of the book, in October 1842, to poet Hannah F. Gould,
"with the kind regards of E. Wheelwright."[8] And his later book,
Traditions of Palestine, resonates with the plot and language of
this earlier one.[9] Ebenezer Wheelwright was the anonymous author of *The Salem Belle*.

Born in Newburyport, Massachusetts, in 1800, Ebenezer
Wheelwright early on became a bookseller in Newburyport and
a flour merchant in Portsmouth, New Hampshire, but he spent
most of his professional life, forty years, as a West Indies merchant in Boston, with particular attention to Santo Domingo.
He was not successful—he acknowledged in his petition for
bankruptcy in 1842 an astounding indebtedness of $33,479.31.
(Perhaps his bankruptcy explains his then publishing anonymously.) Credit ratings made between 1856 and 1874 culminate
with the comment "He is honest enough, but has been poor for
years & hardly makes a living. Has no real basis for cr[edit]."
Wheelwright was married and had three children who lived to
adulthood; he died in Newburyport in 1877.[10]

One obituary writer excused his financial failure thus:
"Himself of sterling integrity, he placed too much trust in the
good intentions of others. This ill-timed credulity neutralized
his considerable business ability, and robbed him of the well-
earned fruits of a life of toil."[11] But that life of toil also included
the literary kind, which, though doubtless not particularly profit-
able, did yield interesting work, particularly the two novels *The
Salem Belle* and *Traditions of Palestine*. Both offer a Christian
piety—in fact, the latter, which includes as an alternate title
Scenes in the Holy Land in the Days of Christ, concerns, in part,
the life of Christ. Wheelwright was a religious man and a "pillar

4 THE SALEM BELLE

in the church." Additionally, he edited a Congregationalist magazine, the *Panoplist*, in 1867 and 1868 and contributed to the *Congregationalist*, finally giving his name, "Eben Wheelwright." Notably, one of his articles in the *Congregationalist*, about evangelical preaching, was reprinted posthumously, slightly trimmed, in the collection *Worth Keeping*.[12] Wheelwright's piety was certainly at odds with the bolder thought of the transcendentalists, but that piety is nonetheless worthy of study. And its presence in *The Salem Belle* confirms that there was a counterpart to the vital tradition that lay beneath the American Renaissance.[13]

The Salem Belle is a short historical novel set primarily in Boston and Salem during 1691 and 1692. It is a work in which a young man, Trellison, who has been disappointed in love, mistakes his wish for vengeance for religious zeal. The basic plot may be set forth briefly. According to an introductory letter, it was based on a story remembered and written down by one "J. N. L." of Cumberland County, Virginia.[14] In Wheelwright's reworking, a Harvard student and a recent Harvard graduate, the upright Walter Strale and the devious Trellison, seek the same young woman, the lovely and devout Mary Graham. Understandably, she accepts Strale and rebuffs Trellison. Hurt and bitter, Trellison seeks revenge. The intensifying witchcraft frenzy in Salem presents him with an opportunity: he can accuse Mary of being a witch.

The Salem witchcraft frenzy was precipitated by young girls' accusations of others, strengthened by supposed confessions, and given credence by ministers, judges, and government leaders. A critical aspect of the event was the belief in "spectral evidence"—that is, that accused people appeared as apparitions and afflicted the accusers. Various explanations of this painful episode in Salem have been offered, including social and political conflict in Salem Village and fear in Essex County owing to the ravages of King William's War (the Second Indian War) in Maine.[15] As a result of the growing persecutions, fourteen women and five men were hanged on Gallows Hill, and one man was pressed to death. This dark event has endured in our literature, most famously in Arthur Miller's 1953 play *The Crucible*, which employs the Salem persecutions to critique the persecutions in the early 1950s of those who may have once had a connection to the Communist Party or who knew people who may have once had a connection. *The Salem Belle* represents an earlier use of the Salem witchcraft debacle, a work that also targets persecution.[16]

The story in *The Salem Belle* is told with a blend of narration, description, and dialogue—this last diminishing as the action increases. Wheelwright presents the conflicting views— the view of reason, articulated by Samuel Willard of the South Church, and that of superstition, argued by Cotton Mather of the North Church—in the novel's central sermons. But Trellison's schemes inevitably proceed. And so, too, do the efforts of Strale and Mary's brother, James Lyford, to rescue Trellison's victim. Strale and Lyford are assisted by William Somers, a devotee of the revered William Goffe, who had passed judgment against King Charles I of England in 1649, had fled England under King Charles II in 1660, and had then lived in Hadley, Massachusetts, where he had been—in this novel, at least—the grandfather of Mary and James. The climax of the novel, set on Gallows Hill, is memorable and compelling.

The tone of the novel is earnest and cautionary—clearly Wheelwright had his "young readers" (*Salem Belle*, 82) in

mind, along with his older ones. There are attempts at comic
relief—interludes with Strale's slave, Pompey—but they are
neither comic nor a relief. And as we may be concerned about
the depiction of Pompey, we should remember that he is one
of many flawed characters in the novel, that he does succeed
in delivering Strale's letter to James Lyford in the snowstorm,
and that Wheelwright himself was antislavery.[17] The burden
of the novel thematically is a serious one: the virtue of piety,
the danger of superstition. It is an explicitly Christian theme,
perhaps closer to the thought of Mary Moody Emerson than to
that of her nephew Waldo.[18] Wheelwright speaks for purity and
simplicity, Providence and the Last Judgment and the hereafter.
He is a Congregationalist, distinct from more liberal Christians,
Unitarians. And Ralph Waldo Emerson, Henry David Thoreau,
Margaret Fuller, and other transcendentalists represent a radi-
cal rethinking religiously, even more liberal than Unitarianism.
Indeed, Emerson wrote in 1841 in "Spiritual Laws" that "the
theological problems of original sin, origin of evil, predestina-
tion, and the like" are just "the soul's mumps and measles, and
whooping-coughs."[19] But Wheelwright's traditional religious
thought is just as sincere and authentic as Emerson's dismissal
of such thought—and it conveys a vital feature of mid-nine-
teenth-century American culture, the context against which
transcendentalism emerged. And the value of traditional religion remains an important issue for twenty-first-century readers.

With well-chosen details and a mix of affection and outrage
concerning early New England, Wheelwright simply and effectively presents a dark time. He deftly blends the historical
and the imagined, at an increasing pace. And he aptly refers to
other texts throughout. Not surprisingly, most of Wheelwright's

references are biblical. The thoughtful and deliberate Willard, in his sermon, fittingly elaborates 1 John 4:1 (King James Version), "Beloved, believe not every spirit" (*Salem Belle*, 110), while the incendiary Mather chooses Isaiah 28:15, "your agreement with hell shall not stand" (113). Earlier, after the earthquake, Mather advises, "The voice we have just heard is the voice of a father telling us to hide in these chambers of his grace, 'until the indignation be overpast'" (Isaiah 26:20; *Salem Belle*, 63). The fanatical Trellison ranges from presumptuously advising Mary about the power of the "Sun of righteousness" (Malachi 4:2; *Salem Belle*, 58) to later plaintively crying, "Accursed be the hour that gave me birth!" (Jeremiah 20:14; *Salem Belle*, 150). Walter Strale notes appropriately, "The wicked flee when no man pursueth" (Proverbs 28:1; *Salem Belle*, 172). And the narrator himself relies on biblical allusion, as when he refers to "hope deferred" (Proverbs 13:12; *Salem Belle*, 53) and to "that inestimable pearl" ("the kingdom of heaven," "one pearl of great price," Matthew 13:45–46; *Salem Belle*, 74). The notes reveal additional biblical references. And the author refers to literary and historical works, as well.

Wheelwright contrasts early Boston to the Boston of his time, the latter with "streets of palaces and walks of state," thus comparing the nineteenth-century city with the elegant Troy of book 6 of Homer's Iliad (*Salem Belle*, 50). He considers "worldly happiness" to be for Mary as alluring as the "song of the sirens," thereby alluding to the enchanting but dangerous voices of the monsters in book 12 of Homer's *Odyssey* (100). He characterizes the tranquil townspeople of Hadley by quoting a quatrain from Thomas Gray's 1751 "Elegy Written in a Country Churchyard," a work that honors those who lived and died in obscurity (82).

And he characterizes Mary in her forest retreat in Salem by quoting lines from William Cowper's 1782 "Retirement," a work that celebrates devout meditation in nature (136). Wheelwright also has occasion to quote from then-recent historical books—with regard to the tree on Gallows Hill, from Abel Cushing's 1839 *Historical Letters on the First Charter in Massachusetts Government* (180); and with regard to the guilt of Chief Justice William Stoughton, from Harvard president Josiah Quincy III's 1840 two-volume *The History of Harvard University* (154). And he cites admiringly the writings of Robert Calef (103), whose 1700 *More Wonders of the Invisible World* was a powerful response to Cotton Mather's 1693 *Wonders of the Invisible World*. For a businessman who had never gone to college, Wheelwright seems to have been pretty well read. And his reading gracefully informs his novel.

Some of Wheelwright's literary techniques are immediately evident. For example, the ominous foreshadowing—the wolf and the wildcat (29), the hurricane (40–41), and the earthquake (62–63), anticipating the tragedy to come—is readily apparent. Less apparent, however, is the formal balance. We may note that the introductory letter speaks of "bold and startling theories, which can only waste the mental energies, and make shipwreck of the mind itself on some fatal rock of superstition or infidelity" and refers to the "Temple," the Bible, as possessing "perfect symmetry" (26). Wheelwright later writes of Judge Samuel Sewall confessing in church, "presenting his own example as a warning to future magistrates to avoid that fatal rock, on which justice and mercy had alike suffered shipwreck" and also of the "perfect symmetry" of the spars of the schooner, the *Water Witch* (153, 158). The phrase "perfect symmetry" calls attention to the verbal symmetry of which it is a part. We may also observe, a bit further in from the beginning of the novel, the appearance of the *Sea Gull*, with Captain Wing, then a foolish escapade involving Pompey (36, 46), and later, a bit further in from the end, another foolish escapade involving Pompey, then the coming of the *Water Witch*, with Captain Ringbolt (128–29, 158). Somewhat closer to the center, Trellison reveals the identity of the woman with whom he had been walking—"The name of the lady . . . is Miss Graham"—and "Walter started at this annunciation" (68); not long after the center, Trellison accuses the same woman of witchcraft—"I pronounce the name of Mary Graham"—and "Mr. Parris started from his seat" (125). And more symmetrical framing is provided. Finally, at the well-framed center—in the ninth and tenth chapters of an eighteen-chapter novel (110–11 and 113–17, respectively)—are the balancing sermons, Willard's and Mather's. These constitute the central fulcrum on which the novel rests. Wheelwright's pride in his rendering of these sermons is suggested by his reprinting that rendering, a set piece, as "A Sabbath in Boston in 1692" in the November 1868 issue of the *Panoplist*.[20]

Wheelwright's first novel received mixed reviews. (For a reprinting of twenty-five recovered reviews of *The Salem Belle*, see appendix B. The page number in the present volume for each quoted passage from a review in this appendix is given here parenthetically.) The one review that seems to reflect a knowledge of the anonymous author is that from the January 1843 issue of the *Pioneer* (a review probably written by editor James Russell Lowell), which begins, "This little novel is, we are informed, the production of a young merchant of this city, whose first attempt in the art of book-making it appears to be" (188). Stating that "the story is one of love, and is pleasingly told" this reviewer was agreeing with some earlier reviewers, who had also praised the work: "The Salem Belle is a simple and beautiful tale, and is beautifully written" (*Boston Evening Bulletin*, qtd. in the *Salem Register*, December 5, 1842, 185), "The style of this little book is easy and graceful" (*New York Daily Tribune*, December 6, 1842, 186), "This story is well and movingly told" (*American Traveller*, December 9, 1842, 187). Yet others disagreed: "We have perused this book as closely as its inordinate dullness would allow" (*Boston Post*, December 5, 1842, 184), "It is an agreeable and entertaining, but not particularly powerful story" (*Knickerbocker*, January 1843, 189), "The present attempt is of a more humble order, and contains some evidences of want of practice or ability in the author" (*Boston Miscellany*, February 1843, 190).

A specific concern was one that Isaac G. Reed had mentioned, anachronisms. Although Reed couldn't find any, the *Boston Post* reviewer complained, "The characters talk just as they do now-a-days" (184–85), and the *Pioneer* reviewer objected to the mention of "lightning conductors" and sentiments suggestive of the "Declaration of American Independence." But this latter reviewer adds, "These, however, do not probably mar the interest of the book to the general reader" (188).

Wheelwright wrote that "True Religion" is "the best antidote against superstition" (*Salem Belle*, 181), and one reviewer observed of *The Salem Belle*, "A highly religious feeling pervades the whole volume" (*Artist*, January 1843, 189). Another reviewer saw the book itself as the antidote: "There are delusions almost as lamentable as that of the Salem Witchcraft which still linger in the land, and it is by way of antidote to such poison that the volume in question is offered to the public" (*Albany Evening Journal*, December 16, 1842, 188). Yet another reviewer saw the book itself as the poison: "If parents wish their children to acquire a taste for novel reading, so that they may be ready to devour every fictitious work that comes in their way, with all the poison it may contain, this is a good work for them to commence with" (*New England Puritan*, December 9, 1842, 187). And some reviewers specifically faulted *The Salem Belle* for presenting the Puritans too harshly: "Those writers who directly or indirectly would stigmatize the faith of the Puritans, never tell us that other men believed and acted in like manner" (*New-York Evangelist*, December 8, 1842, 186); "We cannot help thinking that [*The Salem Belle*] bears too severely upon the motives of some of the eminent divines—Cotton Mather in particular" (*Boston Recorder*, December 30, 1842, 188).[21]

The book enjoyed popularity in its time—it went into a second edition in 1847.[22] And inscriptions in copies of *The Salem Belle* reveal that it was given as a gift from mother to daughter and from friend to friend.[23] Most interesting of all, it was used as a crucial source-text by Nathaniel Hawthorne in *The Scarlet Letter*.

Hawthorne would have known of the book from the reviews—especially the review in the January 1843 issue of the *Pioneer* (one preceded by a positive review of his own *Historical Tales for Youth*). Hawthorne would soon have two of his short stories, "The Hall of Fantasy" and "The Birth-Mark," featured in his friend Lowell's magazine.[24] He might also have learned of the book from Lowell himself and from sister-in-law, bookseller, and book publisher Elizabeth Palmer Peabody. Most suggestively, the publisher of Hawthorne's *Historical Tales for Youth* was also the publisher of *The Salem Belle*: Tappan and Dennet. Perhaps, when Hawthorne visited Boston from Concord in late October 1842, he visited his publisher, at 114 Washington Street, and was told of *The Salem Belle*—and even given a copy. After all, his son Julian wrote, "Some volumes [Hawthorne] bought; but most of them came either as gift copies from their authors, or from Ticknor and Fields, and other publishers." And it is clear that Hawthorne read novels broadly—as his sister Elizabeth stated, "He read a great many novels; he made an artistic study of them. There were many very good books of that kind that seem to be forgotten now."[25]

We do not know what Isaac G. Reed thought of the later chapters of *The Salem Belle*, but we can infer that Hawthorne was attracted to them, for he transformed three passages from these chapters for the later chapters of *The Scarlet Letter*.[26] The first passage from *The Salem Belle* on which Hawthorne drew was that concerning Mary and her brother, James, in her sanctuary in the Salem woods. Sensing Trellison's persecution of her and others' suspicion of her, Mary confides all, and James responds, "Do not sink under this load of sorrow. . . . Deliverance will in some way be effected." Dubious, Mary says, "I would that such a hope could send its reviving influence to my heart" and admits her longing for death. "Why speak so mournfully, dear Mary?" answers James; "This world is not yet a desert, which no flower of hope nor green beauty of summer can adorn." But Mary is disturbed by ominous voices, and "the wind sighed mournfully along, as if in sympathy with the sadness which had fastened deeply on the minds of brother and sister." James tries to reassure her, saying, "Time will soon disclose all; meanwhile, have courage, my dear sister." Still, he warns, "Immediate flight is necessary" (*Salem Belle*, 137–40). We may see that Hawthorne adapted this passage for his purposes. Hester Prynne and the reverend Arthur Dimmesdale, former lovers, meet in the forest outside Boston. Arthur—who has not admitted his part in the affair, as Hester has admitted her own—confesses to her his sense of guilt for his action and for his seemingly false achievement as minister, as well as his hopelessness. Hester reveals what she has not for seven years: that his physician was her husband. Hawthorne writes, "The boughs were tossing heavily above their heads; while one solemn old tree groaned dolefully to another, as if telling the sad story of the pair that sat beneath, or constrained to forebode evil to come." The minister asks, "Must I sink down there, and die at once?" Hester, seeking to bolster Arthur, asks, "Is the world then so narrow? Doth the universe lie within the compass of yonder town, which only a little time ago was but a leaf-strewn desert?" She recommends that he escape to the west or back to Europe, and though he claims, "I am powerless to go," she offers an impassioned encouragement, culminating in "Up, and away!" (*Scarlet Letter*, 189–98).[27]

For this critical passage in *The Scarlet Letter*—the intense meeting of the two lovers—Hawthorne turned to a passage about the intense meeting of a brother and sister in Ebenezer Wheelwright's novel. Supposed witchcraft becomes actual adultery, and the genders of supporter and supported are reversed, but the two passages feature evident parallels in description, in dialogue, and in emotional dynamic. And the resonance that we discern in these passages we may notice again in two additional pairs of passages.

It was the harbor passage in *The Salem Belle* that Hawthorne relied on next, with its focus on the "little schooner," the *Water Witch*, and Captain Ringbolt.[28] Particularly notable is that

Ringbolt is viewed uncertainly in his business practices, yet is nonetheless accepted. Wheelwright writes, "How he obtained his merchandise was sometimes a mystery; but the Salem ladies were careful not to inquire too curiously into the matter; they were quite willing Captain Ringbolt should have his own way; and, as he was uniformly courteous and obliging, any suspicions would certainly be inexpedient, and perhaps unjust. It was rather wonderful, however, that so much charity was extended towards this gentleman, considering the very strict morals of the Puritans, and the rigid honesty with which they were accustomed to discharge their pecuniary obligations." And Somers, who is helping Lyford and Strale in their rescue effort, boards the *Water Witch* to meet with the captain and secure passage for the three in his family (*Salem Belle*, 158–59, 162, 169). Hawthorne adapted this passage effectively. He refers in *The Scarlet Letter* to "a ship [that] lay in the harbour; one of those questionable cruisers, frequent at that day, which without being absolutely outlaws of the deep, yet roamed over its surface with a remarkable irresponsibility of character." It is a "vessel . . . recently arrived from the Spanish main," one that Hester boards to meet with the captain and obtain passage for the three in her family. Hawthorne writes later, "It remarkably characterized the incomplete morality of the age, rigid as we call it, that a license was allowed the seafaring class, not merely for their freaks on shore, but for far more desperate deeds on their proper element. The sailor of that day would go near to be arraigned as a pirate in our own." Yet, he adds, "the Puritan elders, in their black cloaks, starched bands, and steeple-crowned hats, smiled not unbenignantly at the clamor and rude deportment of these jolly seafaring men" (*Scarlet Letter*, 215, 233).

For his treatment of the anticipated escape ship and its men in *The Scarlet Letter*, Hawthorne again turned to a passage in *The Salem Belle*. The correspondence in description, particularly as regards the surprisingly tolerated seamen, as well as a character's seeking passage, confirms the pattern already noticed and invites an expectation of its continuing—an expectation that will be realized in the concluding scaffold passage in both works.

In *The Salem Belle*, when the sheriff tells the crowd gathered at Gallows Hill that the convicted Mary Lyford, "the criminal," has escaped, "Trellison mounted the scaffold." The guilt-ridden accuser, having realized that his seeming religious zeal had actually been personal vengeance, wishes to confess publicly. Wheelwright writes, "His face, which till now had worn the livid hue of death, was covered by the flush of emotion." The crowd is rapt: "Every eye in that immense assemblage was fixed upon him." And he speaks "the feelings which moved his inmost soul." He says that because he had made a false accusation, God "didst turn back upon my soul a tide of guilt and horror" but has now "checked its rage" by permitting this act of atonement. "Hear me, magistrates and men, and ye ministers of an insulted God!" Trellison cries; "hear me, old age, middle life and youth!" And he makes his confession: "I proclaim in your ears that the maiden who has this day escaped death, was guiltless of the crime for which she was condemned to die! Deceived by my own heart, mistaking the bitter passion of revenge for zeal in the service of my Maker, it was this hand that brought down the threatened ruin upon that child of innocence and love." Acknowledging the crimes that had been committed on this hill, he expresses gratitude to God that the planned additional execution did not occur. And after his confession, "the speaker descended from the scaffold" and "passed through the spell-bound and awe-struck multitude." Once he vanishes into the forest, "an unbroken silence reigned for a few moments through all that vast assembly, and the first words that were spoken, were an expression of thankfulness that the innocent maiden had escaped." Yet some people doubt the validity of the confession: "There were not wanting those who attributed this change in Trellison to the power of her magic arts" (174–75).

This, the climactic scene in *The Salem Belle*, was transformed by Hawthorne for the climactic scene in *The Scarlet Letter*. Dimmesdale, having given his Election Sermon, now walks toward the scaffold; his face has a "deathlike hue," but when he stops near the scaffold, his look is "tender and strangely triumphant." He calls for Hester and Pearl, and with Hester's support, he "approach[es] the scaffold, and ascend[s] its steps." The people watch in amazement, "knowing that some deep life-matter—which, if full of sin, was full of anguish and repentance likewise—was now to be laid open to them." "People of New England!" he proclaims; "ye, that have loved me!—ye that have deemed me holy!—behold me here, the one sinner of the world!" Finally, he says, he stands where he should have stood seven years ago. He states that Hester's scarlet letter is only "the shadow of what he bears on his own breast." And "with a convulsive motion he tore away the ministerial band from before his breast." "For an instant," Hawthorne writes, "the gaze of the horror-stricken multitude was concentrated on the ghastly miracle; while the minister stood with a flush of triumph in his face, as one who, in the crisis of acutest pain, had won a victory." And speaking to Hester, Dimmesdale thanks God: "God

knows; and He is merciful!" since he has allowed this atonement, "this death of triumphant ignominy before the people."
When the minister dies, "the multitude, silent till then, broke
out in a strange, deep voice of awe and wonder." Yet some deny
the substance of the confession, saying that the godly minister
had only been suggesting that all men are sinful (250–59).

Hawthorne honored the most extraordinary moment in *The
Salem Belle*, making it, in *The Scarlet Letter*, even more extraordinary. There are differences, of course—the false accusation of
witchcraft as opposed to adultery, life versus death—but the parallels are clear. In this, the third pair of corresponding passages,
the description, speech, and emotional dynamic are powerfully
resonant. Given the correspondences in the two forest scenes,
the two harbor scenes, and the two scaffold scenes, we may well
wonder how Hawthorne might have written *The Scarlet Letter* dif-
ferently had Wheelwright never written *The Salem Belle*.

Our recognizing the presence of *The Salem Belle* in *The
Scarlet Letter* is not merely a matter of engaging in belles
lettres—or perhaps *Belle-Let*—but rather a matter of facilitating
interpretive insight. We may work toward this by wondering why
Hawthorne relied on *The Salem Belle* in the first place.

Wheelwright's authorship of the novel was not generally
known since the work was published anonymously, perhaps
because Wheelwright did not want his creditors to know that
he'd been spending his time writing or to claim whatever mod-
est income he earned from it. Yet the author of the review in
the *Pioneer*, in all likelihood Lowell, seemed to know his identity. Probably Peabody knew his identity. Certainly Hawthorne's
publisher, and Wheelwright's—Tappan and Dennet—knew his
identity. It is fair to conclude, I think, that Hawthorne, well

connected in literary Boston, would have known it, as well. *The Salem Belle* is an engaging book for its theme, its setting, its characters, its language, and its form. Surely, Hawthorne, a student of Puritan history and a former citizen of Salem, would have responded to the work with interest—especially to its view of the inflexibility of the Puritans and the unreliability of spectral evidence. But, I would argue, it is the authorship of *The Salem Belle* that made it particularly important for *The Scarlet Letter*.

A critical clue, I believe, is Hawthorne's twice mentioning Anne Hutchinson in *The Scarlet Letter*. He refers early on to the "sainted Ann Hutchinson" (48), and he later states that without her daughter Pearl, Hester "might have come down to us in history, hand in hand with Ann Hutchinson, as the foundress of a religious sect" (165). Anne Hutchinson was the heroic woman who spoke for the internal evidence of divinity ("Covenant of Grace") over the external evidence of divinity ("Covenant of Works") in what has come to be called the "Antinomian Controversy," lasting from 1636 through 1638.[29] It was one's private sense, Hutchinson argued, rather than public power and wealth, that yielded true religious insight. She thereby challenged Gov. John Winthrop, Rev. John Cotton, and the other leaders of the Massachusetts Bay Colony. In a government founded on religious principles—a theocracy—any religious doctrine inconsistent with the approved doctrine threatened the authorities.

The odd thing is that although Hawthorne twice mentions Anne Hutchinson admiringly in *The Scarlet Letter*, he does not mention her partner in this important episode, a prominent minister and the husband of her sister-in-law, the reverend John Wheelwright. Anne Hutchinson and John Wheelwright are repeatedly linked elsewhere, as in the journals of John Winthrop.

The two bravely defied the theocracy and were tried, convict-
ed, and banished. In this context, the salient fact is that John
Wheelwright was the great-great-great-great-grandfather of
Ebenezer Wheelwright.[30]

Hawthorne was ever attentive to ancestry—he asserted the
sins of his great-great-grandfather William Hathorne and his
great-grandfather John Hathorne in "The Custom-House" introduction (*Scarlet Letter*, 9–10). The former had been involved in
persecuting Quakers, Hawthorne acknowledges, and the latter
in persecuting those accused of witchcraft. Hawthorne might
have added, too, that William Hathorne was a Salem deputy on
the general court that ruled against Anne Hutchinson.[31] This ancestor of Hawthorne and the most famous ancestor of Ebenezer
Wheelwright had been on opposite sides of the Antinomian
Controversy. Aware of Puritan history and genealogy, Hawthorne
would not have missed the rich possibility of a novel about the
Salem witchcraft mania by a writer whose name—never stated—directly linked that writer to Anne Hutchinson's greatest
ally. Persecution for supposed witchcraft in Salem was a type
of the earlier persecution for supposed heresy in Boston. Never
mentioning John Wheelwright in *The Scarlet Letter*, Hawthorne
could nonetheless subtly suggest him by repeatedly alluding to
a work by his direct descendant. So, in this view, not only may
Hester Prynne be associated with Anne Hutchinson, but also
Arthur Dimmesdale may be associated with John Wheelwright.
Hawthorne, I would argue, has offered in his masterwork an allegory of the Antinomian Controversy, with a point of view con-
trary to that of his own ancestor.

This historical event may serve Hawthorne for another allegory. After all, the Antinomian Controversy, one of the earliest

stories in the history of the Massachusetts Bay Colony, concerns
a man and woman who are disobedient to authority and therefore
expelled. Where have we come upon such a story before . . . ?
Patient musing will yield the answer: it is the story of the disobe-
dience of Adam and Eve and their expulsion from Eden. This is
the story that Hawthorne wrote about throughout his career, for
it conveyed his great themes, original sin (consider, for instance,
"Young Goodman Brown" and "The Minister's Black Veil") and
the possibility of redemption. Arthur, whose initials are A. D., is
Adam, and Hester, another name for Esther, is Eve—they represent "the world's first parents [who] were driven out" (*Scarlet
Letter*, 90). *The Scarlet Letter* is, I would argue, a double allegory: with the help of *The Salem Belle*, Hawthorne wrote a historical allegory and a biblical one.

The Salem Belle keenly critiques the fanaticism, the credulity and excess, of Cotton Mather and others. Nonetheless,
it is still a conservative book, espousing reliance on the Old
Testament and the New Testament and traditional Christian
faith. But *The Scarlet Letter* is no book of piety. Clearly Hester
Prynne and Arthur Dimmesdale are sympathetic characters
who have defied Puritan conventions; like Anne Hutchinson
and John Wheelwright, they are subversive. Hester herself became a progressive thinker. Still, the Antinomian Controversy
intimates the story of Adam and Eve. And though "the world's
first parents" are also subversive in defying God, their story is
foundational for any Calvinistic view since it tells of original sin.
Indeed, it was a critical part of the *Westminster Catechism*, which
was so central to Puritan teaching. In view of the link of *The
Scarlet Letter*, by way of *The Salem Belle*, to both the Antinomian
Controversy and, ultimately, the Fall (whether Fortunate or not),

we may recognize anew the ambiguity that Hawthorne conveyed, the blend of the subversive and the conservative that he offered.

Some have claimed that the study of sources is mere antiquarian indulgence. Yet a source may be so significant for critical interpretation of a work that its identification and appreciation are essential. *The Salem Belle* is not just a source for a classic but also, in its valuably aiding our reading, a classic source. Perhaps as long as *The Scarlet Letter* is read, *The Salem Belle* will be read, as well, deepening and intensifying our understanding and our pleasure.

THE

SALEM BELLE:

A Tale of 1692.

BOSTON:

TAPPAN & DENNET,

114 Washington Street.

1842.

INTRODUCTION

The following letter addressed to the author, will explain the circumstances which led to the publication of this little work.

Cumberland County, Va., July, 1841.

DEAR SIR:

In compliance with your request, I now send you a manuscript which contains all the material circumstances of a remarkable legend, founded on the singular events of 1692.[1] The original chronicle is lost, but its general features were strongly impressed on my memory, and I committed them to writing, some years since, and very soon after the discovery that the first manuscript was missing. I hope you will be able to make such use of these materials, as shall expose the danger of popular delusions,[2] and guard the public mind against their recurrence. It is too late to revive the folly of witchcraft, but other follies are pressing on the community,—fanaticism in various ways is moulding the public feeling into unnatural shapes, and shadowing forth a train of undefined evils, whose forms of mischief are yet to be developed. In this state of things, our true wisdom is to take counsel of the past, and not suffer ourselves to be led astray by bold and startling theories, which can only waste the mental energies, and make shipwreck of the mind itself on some fatal rock of superstition or infidelity.[3]

It is an age of boasted liberty and light, but it may well be doubted whether these high pretensions are any powerful defence against popular mistakes. It often happens that the moral plague spot is first seen in the walks of science. It was so in the days which this manuscript commemorates: men renowned for talents and learning gave countenance to a delusion which swept over the land, and will be known in all coming ages by its track of blood and death.

I am not opposed to innovations upon any vicious principle or habit whatsoever. I have no respect for any venerable theory, unless its claims are supported by the Bible and common sense; but how often is that noble edifice of Truth, which the Bible reveals to our eye, deformed by the additions and inventions of men! The Catholic church has for ages thrown up its battlements and towers on the heavenly structure; but these imagined ornaments have only marred its beauty, and hidden its real grandeur from the eye. Other sects have attempted to improve upon the divine Architect; and thus it has happened that the cumbrous scaffolding has fallen, and buried multitudes in its ruins. But if this Temple had been permitted to stand in its own native simplicity, its perfect symmetry,[4] its unrivalled strength and glory, not one of the countless millions who have sought its mysteries would have thus miserably perished.

The elements of delusion always exist in the human mind. Sometimes they slumber for years, and then break forth with volcanic energy, spreading ruin and desolation in their path. Even now the distant roar of these terrible agents comes with confused and ominous sound on the ear. What form of mischief they will assume is among the mysteries of the future;—that desolation will follow in their train, no one can doubt; that they will purify the moral atmosphere, and throw up mighty land-marks as guides to future ages, is equally certain; the evil or good which shall be the final result, depends, under Providence, on the measure of wisdom we may gather from the lessons of the past.

With sincere regard,

Yours truly,

J. N. L.

The foregoing letter speaks for itself; and in conformity to the writer's suggestions, we shall now introduce to our readers the new scenes and hitherto unknown actors in that fatal tragedy, which stains so deeply the history of New England. Follies equally great with those of the witchcraft delusion may yet infest a land as enlightened and civilized as ours; and we cannot agree with our friend in the belief that it is even now too late to revive the same superstition, though its madness may not, as then, terminate in blood. Not more than twelve years since, this same delusion existed in a neighboring state, and within a few miles of its metropolis; numbers visited the spot, and to this day believe that invisible and mysterious agencies controlled the movements of individuals and families.

It is the object of the following pages[5] to hold up the beacons of the past, and in this connection to illustrate the social condition, the habits, manners, and general state of New England, in these early days of its history. We love to contemplate the piety and simplicity, while we deplore the superstition, of those times. Much of the former still remains to challenge our admiration and excite our gratitude; the latter, we trust, is passing away. Our fathers were not faultless, but as a community, a nobler race was never seen on the globe: they were indeed in some degree superstitious and intolerant, but far less so than even the brilliant circles of wealth and fashion they left behind, in their father land; and it will be well for their sons, if they do not stumble over worse delusions, and fall into more fatal errors, than those of their primitive ancestors.

CHAPTER FIRST

THAT BEAUTIFUL SPOT, now known as Mount Auburn,[1] was formerly covered by a forest, which in the early days of New England was the scene of many a startling incident and wild adventure; the wolf howled in its thickets, and the wild cat issuing from its borders, found an easy prey among the flocks of the neighboring farmers: on this account, the utmost skill and energy of the colonists were often taxed, to save their property from pillage and destruction. The young men of those times were bold and expert in the chase, and stimulated by rewards offered by the colony, they often pursued their game many miles from Boston, and seldom returned without trophies of their skill and success. In this way, the vicinity of the town was soon cleared of these scourges of newer and less populous settlements. At the period of our narrative, however, the race of wild animals was not extinct, and the chase was kept up as one of the most agreeable and salutary sports which the austerity of those days would permit.

It was a fine evening in September, 1691, when two young men, who had been engaged all day with a company of sportsmen, were returning leisurely home on horseback. They were both members of Harvard College,[2] room mates and intimate friends. They lingered a mile or two behind their associates, and though travelling after dark was not very safe in those days, yet the beauty of the evening tempted them to loiter, and possibly they were not unwilling to encounter some little adventure, to make up for a dull and unsuccessful chase. At any rate, their conversation was sufficiently interesting to detain them awhile on the road.

'Have you heard from your cousin Mary of late?' said James Lyford to his companion.

'Why do you ask that question? I have no such cousin as you refer to,' replied his friend.

'I have heard you call her cousin Mary,' said James, 'and it was fair to judge from your manner of speaking, that she bore this relation to you.'

'Cousin,' replied Walter, 'is a name that belongs to every body or nobody, as the case may be. It is a very convenient term, and affords a good house to shelter in, when you are bored with questions. I have forty such cousins as Mary.'

'Then you have forty such houses to shelter in,' said Lyford. 'Verily, Walter, you will have no want of inns on the road to matrimony.'

'Forty inns are none too many for a road that promises to be so long, as the one you think I am travelling. To be serious, Lyford, I wish you would let me alone about Mary. She is beautiful and good, but I dare not marry in this Puritan land.[3] I must not reside here; and much as I love Mary Graham, I can never take her to the lighter habits and frivolous scenes of licentious France. You are aware that my parents have left Virginia for Paris; that city must be my home. I must grapple with its temptations, perhaps fall under their power; but duty, honor, nay love itself forbid me to take Mary to its blighting influences. But why talk of such subjects? I am but twenty-one years old and this passion of love, the wise heads say, is not to be depended on; my own feelings may change. And now, Lyford, you have the reasons why Mary Graham must still be my cousin.'

'You speak like a philosopher, nay like a Christian too. I hope your practice will correspond with your precepts, and that you will be careful not to overact the cousin, in your intercourse with Mary. If the cousin in speech becomes the lover in practice and example, it may wake a responsive affection in her own heart, and if so, she cannot quench it, as you may, among the gayeties of Paris. It may fade the bloom on her cheek and quench the light in her eye; but it cannot, like yours, be overcome by excitement abroad, or change at home.'

'Your remarks are very just,' said Walter; 'but why speak in this tone of warning? think you, Lyford, I would trifle with her feelings? I have no evidence that she returns my love; and do you pretend to see ought that is reprehensible in my conduct?'

'Yes, Walter; and if your purposes are not serious in the matter, you ought not to persist in those attentions, which clearly indicate your love to her, and may produce similar feelings on her part. You deceive yourself in this affair, and, it may be, you are deceiving her also. Love is always in advance of the judgment, and you speak like one little acquainted with its snares.'

'And what right have you,' replied Walter, 'to catechise me after this fashion?[4] It is one of your worst faults, Lyford, that you see every thing in a dark and suspicious form. As to Mary, she never suspected me of anything but friendship and good will.

She does not love me. Would to heaven she did! Were it not for the fatal dislike of my parents to this Puritan race, I would rather live with Mary Graham on a mountain fastness, or in the solitude of the desert, than to occupy, without her, the throne of England or France; but my filial duties interpose, and the stern demands of such parents as mine must not be disregarded.'

'Your purposes on this point must be settled,' said Lyford, 'and I must catechise you till they are. I know not that Mary loves you. I hope she never will, until you are so fully sensible of her value and your duty, as to consult her interests in the case, as much at least as your own. If you seek to gratify your vanity, by securing her love, when the obstacles to your union are not to be overcome; then your principles are not firm enough for me, and your friendship is no longer of any value.'

'Ought I to deny myself the pleasure of her society,' returned Walter, 'because the severity of Puritan habits imposes so many restraints, and is so rigid in its inquiries, and exact in its demands? I hope this people, in the march of improvement, will learn to be a little more liberal. You are too severe yourself, Lyford, and all the innocent gayeties of life look to you, as so many clouds between us and heaven.'

'Religion is not severe in her demands,' said Lyford, 'and if she appears so to you, Walter, it is because you invest her with false attributes, and view her through a false medium. Mary Graham is a sincere Christian; her cheerfulness of character you will readily admit; it is a thing of nature, and never runs into excess. She has often had occasion to rebuke the frivolous and turn back the current of levity and folly, and she never shrinks from her duty in this respect, as you well know. I should be sorry to believe any one could command her love, who is not governed by a principle of true religion;[5] and I must add, Walter, if you fail in this point, I hope you will never possess her love.'

'Whence, Lyford, pray tell me, whence this strange interest on your part in Mary? do you mean to stand between us and tell her I am unworthy of her love? You well know I believe in the reality of religion, and reverence it too; you know my character, and cannot suspect me of dishonor. What does all this mean?'

'I mean to put you on your guard, Walter. I can only repeat what I have already said, that your present position and prospects do not warrant you in lavishing upon Mary so many proofs of your love. The course you are pursuing is unjust to her and unjust to yourself. I think you now understand me.'

'I do not understand,' said Walter, 'by what right you prescribe my duties, and undertake to regulate my social intercourse. It would seem to me, to be more wise to mind your own affairs, and let mine alone.'

'And why should I let yours alone, when they interfere with mine? Is it your privilege alone, Walter, to love Mary? Why may I not love her as well as you? She is not less the object of my regard than yours. Mary Graham is more dear to me than I can express. There is no one on earth I love so well. Moreover, she returns my love, and of this I can give you the most unequivocal proofs.'

'Now, I have it,' replied the indignant Walter; 'you mean to supplant me in Mary's love, and all this parade of friendship and religion is a mere artifice to cover your own selfish designs. Lyford, you are playing the hypocrite and the villain.'

'Tell me not thus,' said Lyford calmly. 'Much as I love Mary, I shall not stand in your way. Could I see, Walter, that to all your other virtues, you added that of sincere piety towards God, I should rejoice to see you together at the nuptial altar, and my prayers would go up with yours, that it might be a blessed union.'

'I do not understand you, Lyford: you say I must desist from my attentions to Mary, till my purposes are settled. When I ask why you interfere, you tell me, it is on account of your own love, and then, with strange inconsistency, you add, that, if I was a sincere Christian, you would rejoice in our union. Why do you thus perplex and mislead me?'

'All I have said is true, Walter: the lady you have known by the name of Mary Graham, is the beloved sister of your friend Lyford. It must remain a secret, and you must, on no account, divulge it. Do you now wonder at my love? do you object to my counsels and cautions? This dear sister is not the relative of Mr. Ellerson, with whom she resides. She is my only sister, the grand-child of Gen. Goffe,[6] and was the little companion and solace of his last days. At his death, it was deemed expedient that, under this assumed name, she should reside with her friends at Salem. You have now the cause of my suggestions and warnings. Will you not say they are reasonable and right?'

'You have indeed opened my eyes. Pardon me, oh Lyford! that angry burst of passion which denounced my best friend. It was love to your sister that prompted my wrath; and I must have the forgiveness of her brother, before I can quietly rest.'

'It is forgiven,' said Lyford, seizing the hand of his friend, and together, in silence and tears, they dismounted at the college gate and entered the hall just at the commencement of evening prayers.

CHAPTER SECOND

WALTER STRALE WAS of German descent; his parents, as we
have seen, resided for a time in Virginia, and it was during this
period that Walter was born. When he was about fourteen years
of age, his father determined to remove to France, and establish
a mercantile house in Paris. Mr. Strale, however, was unwilling to educate his son in that gay metropolis; and though by no
means strict in matters of religion, he felt a deep solicitude that
the morals of his child might be preserved. It was at one time
his purpose to leave him in Virginia, among some highly valued
and judicious friends; but as the means of education were very
imperfect in that region, he wisely determined to send him to
Boston, where he knew his studies would be carefully superin-
tended, and his morals effectually guarded.

It was difficult, after all, to understand fully the motives of
Mr. Strale, in sending his son to so rigid a school of morals. He
was a high churchman,[1] and had a thorough contempt for what
he called the superstitions and austerities of the Puritans. It is
probable the extremely volatile temper of Walter made it necessary to place him under careful restraints and a rigid discipline,

and Mr. Strale, who was a man of excellent sense, perceiving
the advantages of a New England education, was willing, for the
sake of its fidelity, to overlook its seeming bigotry and austerity;
for with all his contempt for the Puritan sect, he was ready to
acknowledge, that on the score of integrity and good morals, no
people on earth could rival them.

On the morning of the twenty-fourth of June, 1685, Walter
embarked at James River,[2] on board the *Sea Gull*, a beautiful
schooner, under the command of Capt. Wing,[3] who was a shrewd
trader, as well as a skilful seaman, and had for some time past
kept up a regular intercourse between Virginia and the New
England colonies. He was of course well known to Mr. Strale,
who was entirely satisfied in committing Walter to his care. Mrs.
Strale was careful to furnish her son with every convenience and
luxury which maternal care could provide, and his father sent
with him a negro servant, named Pompey,[4] the most faithful of
all his domestics, and who might in an important sense be called
the steward of his house: he presided over sundry departments
of domestic economy, and no one on the plantation was more
jealous of his rights, or displayed in a higher degree, the pride
and authority of station; yet Pompey professed to be a thorough
democrat, and insisted that all men were born free and equal:[5]
he could never solve the problems and mathematics of slavery,
yet as he required the strict obedience of those under his control, he thought it no more than right to be submissive, in his
turn, to the mandates and discipline of his master.

Pompey's theory of universal liberty exposed him to much
censure from his fellow slaves, for he was in fact a tyrant on as
large a scale as circumstances would permit. Whenever he had
a chance to exercise his love of power, Pompey assumed the

kingly prerogative, and claimed for his opinions the supremacy of law; if any one questioned his authority, or chose to plead his natural rights,[6] Pompey assured him that democracy always consulted the general good, and as power must reside somewhere, it was natural to suppose that he who possessed it knew best how and when it was proper to exercise it.

There was another circumstance which gave Pompey a little extra consequence: in consideration of his fidelity, he was assured that if he continued faithful till Master Walter was educated, he should then receive his freedom. This period was now approaching, and he thought it no harm to take a little of his future liberty in advance; but he often misjudged in regard to the extent of his privilege, and was of course subjected to some slight rebukes, which occasionally left marks on his person, not at all to his credit. If there was any thing to which Pompey had a mortal aversion, it was to the cane or the lash: not, as he said, that he minded the pain,—but they always disfigured a gentleman, and his freedom would not be worth having, if he carried on his person such tokens of his vassalage and debasement.

The first impressions of a sea life are uniformly disagreeable. The pleasant dreams which gather over the mind, in its views of distant countries, changing latitudes, and the thousand forms of beauty which flit through the air, or skim over the water, are dispelled by a single hour's experience, and perish at the first touches of reality. It was so with Strale. He had no proper notion of the unsettled life of a sailor: the splendid visions which hung over the future, were soon scattered by the fatal sea-sickness, and the retreating phantoms thronged around the scenes of home, and invested every locality with the same beauty which at first beckoned him away; but there was no hope of return: the fine southern breezes were wafting him to a strange land, of which he had few correct notions, and whose customs and habits, however repugnant to his feelings, must be adopted as his own.

For two days our little hero was struggling with all the demons of sea-sickness, home-sickness, and the remembrances of past enjoyments; but his mind was too buoyant to continue long under this depression. On the third day he appeared on deck; and as the graceful schooner with fine breezes and under a cloud of canvass was gliding on her path, the bright and the beautiful again adorned the prospect, and restored the pleasures which had been so suddenly and rudely dispersed. He was now able to climb the mast, and take his post on its highest elevation. Walter was always on the look-out for adventure, and the novelties of the sea began to occupy his mind, and invest the objects around him with unwonted attractions. Moreover, Capt. Wing, like other seamen, was graphic in his descriptions of hair-breadth escapes, and was never at a loss for some real or invented tale of wonders. This was an unfailing source of amusement, and Walter listened to his narratives with enthusiasm and delight: he longed for some experience in the same school; he wished to be familiar with dangers, to conquer whatever element might oppose him, and to be in all respects the master of his own destiny.

'There is no character like that of a sailor, Walter,' said Capt. Wing, as they were sitting together near the companion-way, after dinner; 'he is a cook, a seamstress, a washwoman, a gentleman, a philosopher, and an astronomer.'

'You judge from your own crew,' said Walter, 'for you have trained them to all these different characters; but as to the mass of seamen, you might safely add, they are spendthrifts, drunkards, and fools.'

'You are an ignorant boy, Strale. Do you not know there are as many spendthrifts, rowdies, and scoundrels, on shore, in proportion to their numbers, as on the sea? They have a better chance to keep out of sight, and there is a little more refinement in their vices; but after all, the sailor has more good qualities to counterbalance his bad ones: he is grievously slandered by all sorts of men; as a body they are faithful, obedient, patient and generous, and when you take into view their sufferings and temptations, it is wonderful they do so well.'

'The name of a sailor was once full of terror to me,' returned Walter, 'for in every narrative of piracy I have read, they are fearful agents, and seem to commit murder with as little scruple as if it were lawful business.'

'So you have judged of the sailor's character from the worst portraits you can find. This is not fair, Walter: if you take this method with landsmen, you will dread them as much as you do the sailor. What do you think of those land pirates, who decoy seamen into their dens of wickedness, and then turn them houseless and penniless upon the world? There are good and bad in all classes: when you are older, you will do justice to the sailor.'

'I would do it now, Capt. Wing. My judgment was hasty and my language rash; my observation must be more extended before I can be a competent judge in this matter; but in the variety of character you have given the sailor, you have placed things so much at opposites, that I must ask you to unriddle the paradox.'

'The necessities of the sailor,' returned Capt. Wing, 'have made him a little of every thing. You can well enough understand why he acts the tailor or the cook, but you cannot connect these humble offices with the higher qualities of the gentleman and philosopher. Now here is Le Moine—our French steward; no one can be more skilful in his office, and yet that lad can tell you the name of every prominent constellation, and with the proper instruments he can measure his latitude with unfailing accuracy. The same is true of many other seamen, upon whom a careless observer might turn an eye of indifference or contempt. But look, Walter! the clouds are heaving up in the west; we shall have a thunder squall, and you will now see how the Sea Gull dances on the water. That is the black flag,'[7] continued Wing, addressing Roberts, the mate; 'there are pirates in the clouds as well as on the water, and old Neptune[8] gets all the plunder; but the wind is fair, and we can run half an hour before we are overhauled.'

'It grows dark already, and the wind lulls,' said Roberts; 'this sky-scraper will board us directly.'

'Let him come,' said Wing; 'he is one of my old acquaintance, but his dress is darker than usual, and he looks more rough and surly than is his wont.'

The wind had now died away, and there was a perfect calm on the water; the Sea Gull was flapping her wings, but had no onward motion. In a few moments the cloud suddenly expanded, and stretched a curtain of terrific blackness from the western limit of the horizon to the extreme north; the air was now excessively sultry, and an ominous silence and gloom hung over the water; it was presently interrupted by a sharp flash of lightning, followed by a deafening peal of thunder. 'Get up the chain, Mr. Roberts,' said Wing;[9] 'the lightning will soon be in chase of us, and we must throw it overboard.' The chain was instantly run up to the mast head, and its lower extremity hung over the taff-erel; the sails were furled, except the foresail, which was closely reefed, and under a light breeze the schooner again made some headway.

The whole atmosphere was now veiled in blackness, and as if conscious that some terrible convulsion was at hand, the crew of the schooner stood at their posts in perfect silence, while Capt. Wing paced the deck, with that hurried and tremulous motion, which indicated the anxiety that oppressed him. A few drops of rain now fell on the deck and the surrounding ocean. Another and more vivid gleam of lightning, followed by rapid and still fiercer flashes, announced that the crisis was at hand. The next moment the little Sea Gull was enveloped in a blaze of lurid fire, and she staggered under a shock, which but for the chain at the mast head, would have sent her to the bottom; at the same moment, the roar of the hurricane was heard in the distance, and before the panic occasioned by the lightning had subsided, the foresail was torn from the bolt ropes, and scattered in shreds upon the sea,—and in a cloud of tempest and foam, the Sea Gull was rushing through the water, at the rate of ten knots per hour. The sea and sky were now mingled together in wild and terrible uproar; the constant blaze of lightning, the rapid peals of thunder, the trembling and creaking of the schooner as she dashed on her way, presented a scene which startled and overawed even her daring and experienced commander. But the crisis was soon past, and in the course of forty minutes the violence of the squall was over, and before sunset the Sea Gull, with no other damage than the loss of her foresail, was gliding over the water, with a pleasant breeze from the south.

'I am willing to grapple with anything but lightning,' said Wing, 'thanks to the chain we sent up; but for that, Walter, we should have slept to night in the ocean.'

'I must go beyond second causes, Capt. Wing, for such a wonderful deliverance as this; our gratitude is due to a higher Power, and I would never forget it.'

'A sailor's gratitude, Walter, does not often express itself in words, but its impulses are not the less strong because they are invisible.'

'They are transient, however,' said Walter, 'and the occasion that gives them birth is forgotten as a dream. Gratitude must be a steady principle, and not a blind emotion; its fruits must be visible in the life.'

'We sailors,' said Wing, 'are not preachers; we do not study the items of theology; if we did, we should be poor navigators. You are a boy, Strale, and have seen little of the world; a few more tramps over its rough surface, and you will think nothing of these narrow escapes.'

Walter did not reply, but resting on the tafferel, and casting his eye over the fading light of a gorgeous sunset, he traced the beautiful images of a better land, and breathed an earnest prayer that he might be fitted to enter at last upon its pure and everlasting felicities.

No other incident of importance occurred, and on the evening of the third of July, the schooner was moored by the side of a little island off the harbor of Boston. The boat landed Walter and some of the crew by the side of a fine rivulet which flowed from the rock. The quiet evening soon gathered around, and was occupied in grateful recollections of the past, and bright anticipations of the morrow. The antiquary may be interested to know that all which remains of that green spot where Roberts and the young Virginian rambled by moonlight, may be found in the rocks now called 'the Hardings.'[10]

At sunrise on the following morning, the fourth of July, the Sea Gull was again under way. The day was fine, with a clear sky and a soft southern breeze. The schooner glided among the beautiful islands of the inner harbor, which were then filled with trees, and vocal with the songs of birds. It was not, as now, covered by vessels of every name and from every clime, but along its still waters the little galley with oars, the fisherman's skiff, and now and then the white pinions of some taller bark, were seen to move over its silence and solitude; neither did that halo of glory which now circles the birth-day of freedom[11] kindle the patriot's ardor; nor did the stripes and stars wave on the green hills, nor the merry peal of bells go up with the rejoicings of a liberated nation; yet the elements of all this glory were there, and many a prophetic eye even then discerned its dawn upon the mystic horizon of the future.

As the vessel approached the town, the eye of Walter roamed in delight among the varied scenery which adorned the prospect. The islands with their forests, the bay, the blue mountains on the left, were reposing in the beauty of the morning, and the youthful fancy of Strale threw around them a thousand visions of future bliss. On the west the tower of Harvard Hall[12] rose in the distance, shadowing forth that eminence and literary fame, which have since adorned that noble institution. In a few moments, the town with its white edifices, the spires of its churches, its trees and gardens, which had for some time appeared in beautiful outline, were displayed in distinct groups and figures; and Walter, who had till then seen only a few scattered habitations, gazed with intense gratification on the miniature city, as it stretched its little outposts, its convenient and spacious wharf, its thirty sail of merchantmen and coasters, and its eight hundred buildings, with all the attractions of novelty on his eye.

The beauty of the day, the mild breathings of summer, and the carol of innumerable birds, were but the emblems of that sublimer glory, which in after times rested on the birth-day of freedom. The fathers of those times sleep in the dust. The sons, too, are silent as the fathers; but on the ears of the third generation the hymn of liberty poured its strains of gladness, and the name of Washington was borne on every breeze and enshrined in every patriot's heart. That name will be revered as long as Virtue herself shall be loved and honored; and in any future struggle for liberty, his grateful country will interweave with every fold of her star spangled banner,[13] the beautiful motto:

'He led the fathers and inspires the sons.'[14]

CHAPTER THIRD

DURING THE PASSAGE of the Sea Gull up the harbor, no one seemed to enjoy the genial influences of the day more than Pompey: there was something in the very atmosphere, he said, which gave him life and freedom, and he blessed the good land where a man might speak his mind without fear of a cuff or a whip. His fancy revelled in new dreams of liberty, and his exclamations of delight were so frequent and loud, that Walter at last sent him below. Presently, however, his head peered above the companion-way, and on his promise of silence and decorum, Walter permitted him again to come on deck—but it was all in vain. Pompey was in too warm a glow to keep still, and becoming once more a little too garrulous, Capt. Wing seized a rope, but before he had a chance to apply it, Pompey, who saw his purpose, was up the ratlings and on the cross-trees, where, although he had a better view of the blessed land, his raptures soon subsided, and he was enabled to keep silence long enough to insure his safety when he came down.

The schooner soon reached the wharf, which at that time was the great depôt of trade and commerce. As Walter passed by

the long ranges of wooden buildings which then occupied the
ground, the merry cries of the market men, the grand display of
merchandise, and the bustle of wagons and carts, formed a scene
so full of novelty and attraction, that he lingered for an hour or
more, surveying the different objects with lively curiosity and
interest. Pompey was utterly amazed. 'What sort of world be this,
Massa?' was his exclamation, as he stood at the termination of
King street,[1] from whence, at that time, all the business part of
the town was visible. 'Mind your business, Pompey,' said Walter,
'and follow me with the luggage; if you stare at this rate, they
will have you up for a vagabond, and with good reason.' Walter
kept on, but in a moment or two, he heard a shout of merriment
and glee, which had the effect of stopping all business within its
circle. Pompey had just met with one of his own color, and when
the two friends rushed together, it caused such an explosion of
good nature, as sent the laugh up and down the street: the idlers
came out to gaze, and a stout drayman,[2] who saw the ludicrous
attitude of the two blacks, tripped them both into the gutter, when
Pompey, covered with shame and choked with dust and passion,
rose on his feet and gave the drayman a violent blow, which
nearly felled him to the ground; he was then seized by an officer and carried to prison on the charge of fighting in the streets;
a serious crime, and one for which the fathers of New England
had provided due punishment, which was usually inflicted in full
measure on the culprit; for the rigid justice of those days was not
often tempered by the mild pleadings of mercy.

Walter saw how the affair was going, and wishing his servant
to have the full benefit of such a lesson, did not choose to interpose, but directing a porter to take his luggage, he saw Pompey
move off to prison, with no regret that the ridiculous farce, in

which he had acted, was likely to meet its proper rebuke. On his arrival at the hotel[3] he was provided with suitable lodgings, and spent the remainder of the day in walking about town, and viewing the various objects of interest it contained.

The morning of the next day was occupied in visiting some of the gentlemen of the town, to whom Walter was furnished with letters. Among these were Mr. Stoughton, Judge Sewall, Rev. Mr. Willard, and Mr. Winthrop,[4] the latter a distinguished practitioner at the bar. He was welcomed with the warm hospitality of those days, and assured of their kind offices and best efforts for his welfare. He related to Mr. Winthrop the affair in King street, between the two Africans, who caused an immediate examination of the case before a magistrate, which resulted in the release of Pompey, who followed his master home. His dream of liberty had by this time nearly vanished, and the poor negro was deeply concerned at his disgrace.

'It was a great breach of good manners, Pompey, to make such a noise in the street and tumble about in the gutter,' said Walter; 'I thought you intended to act the gentleman.'

'So I did, Massa, and many is the gentleman I have seen in the gutter, besides me.'

'Very well, he is no gentleman while there, especially if he clamors and fights as you did. That was too vulgar even for a gentleman's servant, and I was ashamed to have the public see you had not been better trained.'

'It is hard to get into jail, Massa, for being so glad to see an old friend. Is it one of the laws, Massa?'

'It is every where a law, to pick up vagabonds in the gutter,' said Walter; 'if you put me to this trouble every day, I shall send you back to Virginia.'

'Right glad to go, Massa; homesick enough,' said Pompey.

'Well, you must get over it, and behave in better fashion for the future. I am not without hopes, you will learn good manners in due time. This lesson will help you a little, and so will I, if you will try to help yourself. I want you now at my lodgings, and will there show you what you have to do.'

Pompey followed Walter to the inn, in better spirits; for a word of encouragement always gave him a glow of happiness, and he tossed his head with a new sense of his importance, as he entered the hotel to receive the orders and wait upon the movements of his young master.

In a few weeks, Walter was received into the family of Mr. Gardner, a highly respectable merchant, who was a friend and correspondent of his father. In this situation he was favored with the best literary advantages and possessed every facility for social enjoyment. He was committed to the special care of Mr. Cheever,[5] one of the best teachers New England has ever produced, and made rapid proficiency in his studies; in less than two years, he was fully prepared for college; the usual examination was passed with singular credit, and he entered Harvard University in the year 1688. The social and moral influences which had surrounded him in Boston had done much to check his too volatile disposition, and to inspire him with a high respect for the consistent and exemplary piety which so much prevailed in those days; he was freely admitted to the best circles, where elegance without ostentation, cheerfulness without frivolity, and refinement without the despotism of fashion, were the natural and graceful ornaments of the social character.

Walter was not slow in improving the advantages he enjoyed. It is true, he sometimes thought the bow was bent too long, and that the demands of religious duty might be somewhat relaxed, yet he had the good sense to perceive in the state of the community around him, the best illustration of the excellence and moral force of that education in which science and religion acted in concert and moulded the temper and habits by their combined influence. Walter, however, was not religious in the true sense of the term. His understanding admitted the excellence of the moral precepts that were taught him, and his conscience confessed their power. He wanted neither light nor conviction on the subject, but he had no special love for the strict requirements of religion and had no experience of its renovating power on the heart.

We must now pass over the first years of college life, and pursue the train of incidents up to the period which introduced our narrative. Walter had attained his senior year in college, and had proceeded thus far with credit to himself and the esteem and confidence of his instructors. He had now reached that period when the character is rapidly developed, and new forms of good or ill are daily stamped on its features. At the age of twenty years, with a graceful person, pleasing manners, and confessedly in the highest literary ranks, his prospects were too flattering to escape the fears of his friends, that the temptations of life might prove too strong for his principles; but those fears were groundless. Although every distinction which wealth or talents could bestow were at his command, yet Strale was never unduly elated; there was no affectation of superiority, no arrogant assumption of rank, no pride of distinction. His whole course at Cambridge had been marked by a strict regard to his moral and social duties. He had even declined the personal services of Pompey, who was left in the family of Mr. Gardner, and chose to perform himself the little drudgery of college rooms, and to live in commons upon the ordinary college fare. The uniform kindness of his temper, his liberality to his fellow students, and his strict regard to every point of order and discipline, procured for him an enviable and well deserved reputation.

It was happy for Strale that among his youthful associates he possessed such a friend as Lyford. It was still more happy that the female society to which he was introduced, possessed every moral ornament, as well as the graces of refinement and good breeding. Among the ladies of New England he found very much to respect and admire. A scrupulous regard to the delicacy and dignity of the sex was almost universal, nor is it to be denied, that in personal attractions and all the truly valuable ornaments of character, they have not been surpassed by any succeeding generation.

It is pleasant to call up the beautiful pictures of simplicity and grace which adorned the dwellings of our ancestors; to look back upon those groups of maidens, who breathed the air of moral purity, and bounded in the full tide of health and happiness, over the gardens and among the forests of this very spot, where the city now spreads its marts of business, its solid piles of masonry, its 'streets of palaces and walks of state.'[6] If the beauty of that moral painting was sometimes marred and defaced, it was as often retouched by many a simple, yet unconscious artist, and its calm and beautiful outline is still visible as a blessed vision of the past, and a sure beacon to future eminence and glory.

It was common among the students of Harvard College in those days, with the approbation of the faculty, to make frequent visits to Boston for purposes of social and religious improvement. This practice was encouraged in the belief that the early habits of the students would be formed on the best models, and that the moral feeling which then prevailed, was just the atmosphere in which they should live and breathe. The elder Mather,[7] at that time President of the College, was himself a resident of Boston, and in connection with his College duties, was pastor of a large congregation in town. The students were, of course, when in Boston, much under his supervision, and any instance of misconduct would hardly escape the notice of this vigilant guardian of the public morals.

It was at the house of Mr. Hallam, a gentleman of intelligence and wealth in town, that Strale first met with the young lady whom we must still call Miss Graham. She was the intimate friend of Miss Caroline Hallam, a beautiful and accomplished girl of the same age. The early friendship they had formed was of a character not readily to be interrupted, and the interchange of visits between Boston and Salem was kept up, as often as the circumstances of the two friends would allow. There was, however, a strongly marked difference between the two young ladies. Miss Graham was sincere, confiding, and transparent in her character. Miss Hallam was somewhat vain, unusually gay in her temper, and strongly inclined to suspicion and jealousy; yet these points of character were not sufficiently developed, to interrupt the harmony which had prevailed for several years. In the summer of 1690, at a small musical party at Mr. Hallam's, Walter was first introduced to Miss Graham, and the sudden and powerful interest she then acquired in his affections, had never been subdued. From that time, when Mary was in town, the house of Mr. Hallam was Walter's chosen resort. His attentions, however, were cautiously shunned, and while she never failed in all the forms of politeness, there was a manifest reserve in her manners, which, though it checked his hopes and increased his respect and admiration, did not at all diminish his love.

It was not surprising, however, that Mary should feel some interest in a young gentleman of so many accomplishments, as were possessed by Strale. But, while she was careful not to betray any special attachment, or discover to her friends that her affections were at all involved in the matter, and while perhaps she was herself unconscious of the power he was gaining over her feelings, the reserve of her manners gradually softened, and she engaged with lively interest in that sportive and animated conversation, for which both were distinguished. But her natural seriousness of manner inclined her rather to subjects of graver import, and she never concealed the fact that religion and its kindred themes, were those upon which she most delighted to dwell. Indeed, this was so obvious to Strale, that he often regretted that his own heart refused its sympathy with a subject, which was uppermost in the heart of the object of his love. It was plain, however, that the acquaintance of the parties was becoming every day more agreeable, and the general opinion was, that, if the holy bands of matrimony did not finally unite such kindred tastes and tempers, no predictions, touching these matters, could ever be trusted again.

This state of things between the parties continued for about a year, when it gave occasion for the conversation which Lyford held with Strale on their return from a hunting excursion. A few days after this, Walter informed Lyford he had written his father of his attachment to Mary, and desired permission to make known his feelings, and, if she did not object, he requested his consent to their future union. This letter was accompanied by one from Mr. Gardner, in which he assured Mr. Strale that Miss Graham was every way worthy of Walter's love, and possessed all those graces and accomplishments which would reflect the highest credit on the family.

This declaration on the part of Strale was entirely satisfactory to Lyford, and he no longer objected to the occasional intercourse which had been kept up between the parties. It is not improbable, however, that Walter was a little in advance of his father's consent, and that some of those visions, which glittered on his eye, would reflect a portion of their brilliancy on the mind of Miss Graham. But nothing was said of a definite character, and the two friends were left to the pleasure attending the consciousness of mutual love and the occasional sadness of 'hope deferred.'[8]

Mary Graham was a decided favorite in Boston. Her personal attractions were surpassed by none, and her manners and conversation were scarcely rivalled by any of her associates. Yet she was simple and unpretending in her demeanor; her religious character, from long reflection and deep conviction, was firm and decided; but she was no enthusiast, and though even Walter, at times, thought her more precise and severe than necessary, yet there was a charm of inexpressible beauty, interwoven with her every movement, a purity of mind and purpose, a visible communion with things unseen and eternal, which commanded the unvoluntary homage and respect of all who knew her.

It was not strange that a young lady thus gifted, should have many admirers, nor that love of equal strength with that of Strale's, should be kindled in the affections of others. Such was the fact in regard to Mary, and its consequences will be unfolded in the progress of our narration. But it is a law of our nature, most beneficent and wise, that but one response can be given, and, when given in sincerity and truth, it is done with no divided heart.

CHAPTER FOURTH

IT WAS A FROSTY and dark evening, early in the following February, when Walter and Lyford went into Boston, to meet a party of friends at the house of Mr. Elliott, a gentleman who had recently come from Europe, and whose commercial operations were, in future, to be conducted with England and her American colonies. Mr. Elliott was wealthy, intelligent and highly respected by all classes. It was deemed a high privilege among the young gentlemen of the town, to be on visiting terms with his family. His son, James, was amiable and agreeable, and Miss Margaret Elliott was a decided belle. The good people of those days were sometimes annoyed by the style of her dress, which was somewhat in advance of the prevalent fashions, and was always formed upon the best London or Paris models, though greatly modified and adapted to the New England taste. Among the younger maidens, she would frequently encounter looks of admiration or envy, according to the taste or temper of the parties. But Miss Elliott insisted she could accommodate herself no further to the prevalent scruples concerning dress, and as she was a most amiable girl, condescending and affable to all, her imagined vanity and love of fashion was generally forgiven.

The large hall of Mr. Elliott's house was brilliantly lighted, and at seven o'clock the company began to assemble. They were received at the door by a servant, and the ladies and gentlemen conducted to different rooms, where the servants assisted in the arrangement of their dresses. On entering the hall, they were received by Mr. Elliott, who presented each to Mrs. Elliott, according to the etiquette of the day, and the parties then dispersed themselves about the room.

When the young gentlemen from Cambridge arrived, the spacious rooms were nearly filled with guests: the beauty and pride of the town were present, members of the learned professions, several clergymen with their families, Governor Stoughton, Judge Sewall and other eminent men of the day, to whom these hours of recreation were among the greenest spots in their lives of professional labor and care; but for the youthful part of the company, these occasions possessed the highest charm. The morning of life, as yet unclouded by care, and spreading its pictures of joy on every hill, and crowning even the distant and snow-clad steeps of old age with a visionary green, was too balmy and bright to be false, too serene and beautiful to be deformed by sudden tempest or a threatening sky. So reasons the mind in its early views of life; such were the hopes and expectations of these young men and maidens, as they looked through the vista of time. Yet was there nothing in the nature of these social enjoyments which might not challenge the scrutiny of even the most rigid and severe. There were no card tables, no merry dances, nor frivolous games; yet conversation was sprightly, good humored, and sometimes gay; the interchange of social courtesies was cordial and sincere, and the mirth of the occasion, if it might be called such, was neither excessive nor unbecoming.

'You can boast the belle of the flowers tonight,' said James Elliott to his cousin, Miss Hallam; 'it seems like a rare exotic, and is a perfect novelty to me; pray tell me where you obtained it.'

'I had it, James,' said Caroline, 'from one of the mountains of the moon.[1] You know our own supply of flowers in winter is very small.'

'You are dealing in riddles, Miss Hallam. Pray explain: I would like to know where more might be had.'

'I have told you, James, already: will you never believe me?'

'Hardly ever, Caroline. You are always shutting the door and leaving me in the dark. It would be civil to give me a lamp, that I might find my way out.'

'You must get out by moon-light, James. I have you told a plain story, and if you will not believe me, why, let it go. You believe, every day, things much less credible.'

At that moment, Miss Graham joined the circle, and James, appealing to her, said he hoped Miss Hallam would give her the explanation she had refused to him.

'Why, you must study your map, Mr. Elliott,' said Mary; 'I suppose the flower, or the plant that produced it, came from Africa.'

'There, James,' said Caroline, 'see how little wit you have! Would you not thank me, now, to shut you up in the dark, to hide your blushes?'

'No, Caroline, for then I could not see you, and as to the blushes you speak of, they will help my looks, which are none of the best. Miss Graham, you have given this little vixen the best of the game: I shall pay up hereafter.'

So saying, James moved off in tolerable humor, and glad to make his retreat. He soon joined another group of ladies, and as his conversation was very agreeable, he seldom found himself without willing auditors. Moreover, he felt that, on the present occasion, the honors of his father's house were in a measure confided to him, and the slight confusion of the incident soon passed away.

The two young ladies he left were joined by another young gentleman from Cambridge, named Trellison. He had graduated the preceding autumn with some reputation; his manners were polished; and, except an occasional harshness of expression, his face was not disagreeable. He made high professions of religion, and there was a seeming modesty and sobriety in his deportment; yet to a practiced eye, he displayed the tokens of fanaticism and hypocrisy rather than the unequivocal signs of frankness and sincerity in his religious faith.

'I believe you always worship at the South church, when you are in town,' said Mr. Trellison, addressing Miss Graham. 'I have never seen you at the North.[2] Will you go with me to hear Mr. Mather next Sabbath, by way of variety?'

'My friends,' returned Miss Graham, 'worship at the South church, and in truth I prefer Mr. Willard's preaching to that of Mr. Mather. He is a man of singular candor, and his calm and benevolent temper has so gained my esteem and confidence, that I think his preaching more useful to me than any other.'

'All this is true of him, and much more; but he is a man who never believes more than he can help, and is very slow to give credit to matters of fact. I think this a serious blemish in his character.'

'Some men,' returned Mary, 'believe a great deal too much. Coolness and caution in all matters of belief are essential to a well balanced mind. If this be a fault in Mr. Willard, it is certainly a very amiable one.'

'This coolness you speak of, Miss Graham, is a great enemy to prompt action. I go for energy and decision; without these features the mind is comparatively powerless, and its great purposes perish in the moment of their birth.'

'You cannot say this of Mr. Willard,' said Mary; 'his caution tempers his zeal, but does not suppress it; his piety is not the less ardent because it is cheerful and unobtrusive.'

'You are quite his eulogist, Miss Graham. I am more inclined to the fervid zeal of the Mathers, than to the quiet course of Mr. Willard. Nevertheless, I esteem him highly. But I believe in the power of mighty impulses to renovate the heart and subdue the evil principle in man. The heart of man is like a wasted garden, full of unsightly plants and noxious weeds, and dry and barren trees. When these are burnt up by the terrors of the Lord, the Sun of righteousness[3] covers it with a beautiful verdure, and it brings forth the fruits of holiness.'

'I believe, as you do, in a supernatural change of heart,' said Mary; 'but I consider a holy life and a willing obedience to the commands of God, as the best evidence of his presence and power in the heart; nor am I sure, that a soil, from which the noxious weed and barren tree have been rooted out, may not as well bring forth the fruits of holiness, when the seed are implanted by a divine hand, as if it were burned over with fire. Nevertheless, there is beauty and truth in your figure, and it is doubtless a consolation to the true believer, to have a vivid remembrance of the work of the law on his heart.'

'Those are certainly the most active Christians,' replied Trellison, 'who see the depths of ruin, from which they have been rescued. They have a clearer view of the danger of their fellow men, and are excited to greater efforts in their behalf. It appears to me the special design and tendency of Mr. Mather's preaching is, to awaken this solicitude and excite to such efforts.'

'The minds of individuals,' returned Miss Graham, 'are affected by such modes of address, as are best adapted to their peculiar habits and tempers. Some men are more readily moved by terror, others by the winning persuasions of the gospel. But in the remarks I have made, do not, I pray you, think me the enemy of Mr. Mather. I am not, and if I had not heard him preach, it is quite probable I should go with you next Sabbath. I admire his talents, and his literary character is deservedly high. Moreover, he is very agreeable in conversation, and has entertained me much this very evening.'

At this moment, the summons to the evening's entertainment prevented the reply of Trellison. In a large room, adjoining the hall, a range of tables had been laid, and were covered with a rich variety of foreign luxuries as well as the more substantial products of New England. The hospitality of those days was not marked by all those nice refinements, which so often embarrass the social life of the present times; but it was liberal to profusion, and, though simple in its forms, was not deficient in a just regard to the proprieties and restraints of elegant society. Yet there was one feature in the social life of New England, which constituted its principal charm, and gave it a direction to the highest and noblest objects of human pursuit. It was a devout recognition of Providence, at every social meeting, an unembarrassed and grateful thanksgiving, always expected and offered with becoming reverence and a grateful sense of obligation.

This interesting service was performed on the present occasion by Mr. Willard, the accomplished pastor of the South church, and a more pleasing spectacle is seldom witnessed. Around the tables were the fathers of the colony, men eminent for learning, for mental vigor, and above all, for distinguished, consistent and exemplary piety. Mingled among them, in different groups, were fifty young men and maidens, blooming in youth, the flower of the province, the first in rank and manners in the land, all bowing their heads in reverence, while the evening thanksgiving went up to the Giver of all good and the source of every blessing. This was a part of that education which has made New England the glory of all lands. But this glory has passed away from the brilliant circles of its now splendid metropolis; gifts are received with no audible response to the Giver; and Religion is too often deemed a graceless intruder in the walks of wealth and fashion.

The conversation, which had occupied Trellison and Mary, had not escaped the notice of Strale. From some cause, these two young gentlemen were not often pleased with each other. The young ladies insisted that Trellison considered Strale as a rival who could not easily be supplanted. It was plain that Miss Graham was, in some measure, the cause of this dislike; yet apart from this, the characters of the two were so exceedingly different, that little harmony of feeling could be expected between them. Strale was always pleasing. Distinguished for frankness and simplicity, his conversation was vigorous, playful and strongly marked with the characters of truth and propriety. Trellison was cautious, frequently reserved, with good manners; but an expression of cunning, and even malignity, would often cross his countenance, and give to his features, which, in general, were pleasing, a harsh and disagreeable aspect. He was selfish and very suspicious of the motives and doings of others, and his bad temper towards Strale was often manifested by an ambiguous politeness, throwing off sarcasms, mingled with civility enough to show his own dexterity, and conceal, in part, the bitter hatred which prompted him.

At the supper table Walter found means to join Miss Graham, and the conversation, as usual, soon became playful and animated. Several young ladies gathered round and formed a circle of attraction, which, wherever it moved, was sure to carry its satellites with it, and keep up its brilliancy. Trellison who had made unusual efforts to be agreeable, finding himself unable to break the circle by starting new topics and diverting the current in his own favor, at last joined it himself. Soon after, as Walter was passing a glass of wine to Miss Graham, Trellison's arm, either by design or a sudden change of position, struck the hand of Strale and overturned the wine upon the dress of Miss Graham. Trellison stooped to take up the broken pieces, remarking:

'How unfortunate! what was the matter, Mr. Strale?'

'I ask pardon, Miss Graham,' said Strale; 'wine, they say, is a mocker; but I would rather its color might grace your cheek than stain your dress; my hand is not usually unsteady. Perhaps Mr. Trellison can explain why it is so to-night.'

'I am sorry you think any explanation due from me: what possible connection could I have with the accident? Mr. Strale, your imputation is rude and unjust.'

'I know not how it is, Mr. Trellison: some person's arm struck my hand abruptly, as it seemed to me. I thought it was yours: but if you disclaim it, I am willing to take back the suspicion, and think it an accident.'

'Your apology is hardly in season,' said Trellison; 'you had no right to suppose any one in this room would willingly help you stain a lady's dress; still less, to point out an individual, in a manner so invidious and selfish.'

The young ladies, who had been engaged in assisting Miss Graham, now returned, and before Walter had opportunity to reply, Miss Hallam remarked to Trellison, that he was a very careless gentleman to molest a lady's cup-bearer. Strale looked at Trellison, who bore this rebuke unabashed; but he instantly replied: 'I am sorry you think me so careless, Miss Hallam; but indeed, I was not aware of any agency in the matter.'

'It may not have been intentional,' said Miss Hallam: 'it could not have been, and perhaps I was deceived in supposing it to be you; nevertheless, I thought it was.'

The conversation was getting a little too grave, and a movement towards the hall was readily seconded by some of the young ladies, and the company adjourned to the other room. The impressions which this conversation made were not of the most agreeable kind; but they soon passed away, and other topics and amusements restored, at least in appearance, the harmony which had been so rudely disturbed.

The festivities of an evening party were always closed, in those days, by devotional exercises; and on the present occasion, they were performed by the younger Mather, who was now in his early manhood, and whose vigorous, yet credulous and superstitious mind was destined to exert a powerful, and we must add, a baleful influence upon the social condition of the colony. It happened that, as he was about to read the evening hymn which preceded the closing prayer, the shock of an earthquake[4] was slightly felt by the company. It was immediately followed by a rapid and tumultuous sound, like the rattling of heavy wheels over the pavement. Another shock succeeded, and the house, for an instant, rocked, as if a sudden whirlwind had passed by. In a moment, all was hushed, and the awestricken party stood like motionless statues, wrapped in amazement and terror.

The silence, which lasted a moment or two, was broken by Mr. Mather, who remarked that the providence of God had furnished a theme for reflection, which was fitted to impress the mind with the instability of earth and all earthly things. It was a voice of admonition which could not be disregarded. When pestilence and famine were abroad in the land, the means of at least temporary relief were possessed. But when the pillars of the world were moved and its foundations upheaved by unseen and terrible agents; it was then every earthly refuge was vain. 'But,' he continued, 'there is one hiding place which, in the midst of every convulsion, is safe for the believer. Time has not reached it with his consuming hand; tempests have beat upon it in vain; pestilence, famine or earthquake can never waste its strength; it shall survive the ruin of earth, the wreck of planets, and a dissolving universe. This refuge is the 'Rock of ages;'[5] here are towers of strength and palaces of hope, built on foundations which rest on the throne of God. The voice we have just heard is the voice of a father telling us to hide in these chambers of his grace, 'until the indignation be overpast;'[6] it is but a louder echo of his mercy, warning us that earth must pass away with a great noise, and the elements melt with fervent heat; and, at the same time, assuring us that, though the mountains depart and the hills be removed, his loving kindness shall not depart from his people.'

Such was a part of the extempore address, which the interesting circumstances of the evening called forth. It was followed by a fervent prayer, and a train of salutary reflections occupied the minds of the party, as they dispersed to their several homes.

CHAPTER FIFTH

'WHAT AN UNFORTUNATE evening we have had!' said Strale to Lyford, on their return home; 'every thing has gone wrong. Trellison was in the wrong place, the wine went the wrong way, and the earthquake came at the wrong time.'

'Hush, Walter; you speak too lightly on this latter point. All the trifles of the evening vanished from my mind when the earthquake voice of my Maker spoke to me of a coming judgment, and a crashing world. Why is it, Walter, that we think so little of our future destiny? Why do we build our hopes on a world we must leave so soon?'

'I know it is a fitting time to think, James,' said Strale; 'I would that sensible objects had less effect upon me; but so it is, Lyford, and I cannot help it. I thought more of my own misfortunes this evening than any thing else. Even the earthquake scarcely diverted my thoughts from that unfortunate overthrow, which I verily believe was caused by Trellison.'

'It is vain and foolish, Walter, to dwell upon such trifles. I am no enemy, as you well know, to social pleasures, but at such an hour as this, I am sorry your mind is not better occupied. It is now nearly midnight, the way is solitary, and its very silence seems to me ominous and impressive: these leafless trees, all nature hushed and dead, the voice which has just issued from the groaning earth,—all these speak to us of our mortality, warn us of the flight of time, and throw around us the dim figures and solemn images of a coming hereafter.'

'You are superstitious to-night, James. I do not mean to say your views in the main are not reasonable and right, but there is a tinge of melancholy in your language and manner, which is hardly natural. I wish to be as religious as you are, but not quite so grave, for gravity you know has little to do with my constitution. We are now nearly home, and when we get there I will converse with you on religion if you wish, but not exactly in this way.'

At this moment they entered a narrow turn in the road, which was lined on either side by a dense forest for nearly a mile; the large tangled bushes formed the only fence, and the way was so nearly open, that any one coming from the woods might enter it with little obstruction. The night was extremely dark, and not even a star was visible; the young travellers, however, were provided with a small lantern, which was a very important guide in this stage of their walk. A slight rustling in the woods had once or twice arrested the attention of James, who remarked that he could hardly account for it at that hour of the night, and at this season of the year.

'The wind may produce it,' said Strale; 'the imagination may produce it; and possibly, Lyford, the Salem witches may be dancing about in the woods. By the way, I wonder Cotton Mather said nothing about these rumors from Salem; he is just the man to believe them. Do you think it possible he knows nothing of the story?'

'Very possible, indeed; for it attracts very little notice, and is in fact very little known. Mr. Mather is inclined to superstition, but I hardly think he believes in ghosts and witches. I am quite sure his father would not sanction such folly, and the father and son are not much inclined to differ in opinion.'

'I have no very high opinion of Cotton Mather. He may be a good man; he is certainly forcible and impressive in the pulpit; and it is thought his rising greatness will soon eclipse that of his father; but in my belief Dr. Mather, if not a greater man, is a far better one, and the son, with all his eccentric brilliancy, can never rival the father. He is headstrong, violent, and intolerant. I hope the President will soon return, and keep his son from meddling with college affairs.'

'He will soon be here,' said Lyford; 'and in my opinion he will come the messenger of good to these colonies; he will obtain for this Puritan community from the Prince of Orange, what the bigotry and pride of the Stuarts would never grant.[1] No man's return to Boston can be so welcome as that of Dr. Mather.'

The conversation was interrupted by a sound in the woods, resembling the tread of footsteps among the tangled bushes. Walter proposed to walk in the direction indicated by the noise, and ascertain if possible the cause. Lyford, however, objected, and thought it best not to separate; for a little of the superstition which such circumstances might readily occasion, had now affected the minds of both, but particularly that of Lyford. They walked silently along for a moment or two, when a sudden flash was seen, which was followed by a quick, sharp report, like that of a rifle, and the rustling of the bushes over the way indicated that they were torn and rent by a shower of lead. Another flash succeeded, when a shot struck the hand of Strale, and passed off into the neighboring woods.

'There are no witches here,' said Strale; 'there is too much cold lead to come from the gun of a witch; look at my hand, Lyford, and be thankful as I am it was not my head.'

'This is no time to look at heads or hands,' said Lyford, 'but to escape the loss of both, if we can,' and he instantly extinguished the lamp, and suppressing the voice of Walter, who was about to speak, they moved along as silently as possible, and in half an hour entered the college gate.

These singular events, following each other so rapidly, made a strong impression on the minds of both Strale and Lyford. It was impossible not to connect them in some shape with Trellison, and yet there was a boldness and audacity in the affair, which was hardly consistent with his reputation for caution and cunning. It was too late to do any thing about it that night, and after an examination of the wound of Strale, which proved very slight, a few simple remedies were applied, and they retired for such rest as the exciting scenes of the evening might allow.

The next day the story was rife in Cambridge, and a strong excitement was produced throughout the town. Trellison was at once suspected, and as his dislike to Strale was well known, a legal investigation was proposed, and immediately carried into effect; not, however, without a strong remonstrance from Walter and his friend, who were disposed to let the affair drop. A warrant was immediately issued for the apprehension of Trellison, but before it could be served, he was warned of the movements against him, and advised to make his escape. This he refused to do, and declared himself ready for immediate trial. Accordingly, when the officer appeared, he accompanied him to a magistrate, and the investigation proceeded in regular form.

All the evidence against Trellison was circumstantial, and rested mainly on two facts; one of these was his inveterate dislike of Strale, which, with all his caution, he had been unable to conceal; the other was the very late hour of his return, and his disturbed and agitated manner, which was remarked by several persons, as soon as he entered his lodgings. In his defence, he stated very forcibly his objections to the first branch of evidence, declaring that nothing less than madness could prompt even an enemy to a kind of revenge which was so rash, and must recoil so soon on the aggressor. He explained the lateness of his return by saying that he walked with one of the young ladies for nearly half an hour before he left Boston, and on taking his leave, he came home on the public road, and was himself surprised, on his arrival, at the lateness of the hour.

The magistrate demanded the name of the young lady, as her evidence might be important in the case.

Trellison replied, that he should give it with reluctance, but would do it, if the requirement was mandatory.

The magistrate repeated the question, and insisted on a prompt reply.

'The name of the lady,' said Trellison, 'is Miss Graham.'

Walter started at this annunciation,[2] and the blood rushed to his face; but he recovered himself in a moment, and the sudden flush escaped the notice of all excepting Trellison.

The magistrate thought it necessary to send for Miss Graham, and ordered that Trellison should be held in custody till the next day, when Miss Graham's evidence would be taken, and all the parties should have a fair hearing.

Strale and Lyford now requested that Trellison might be liberated on his own bail. They also stated the complaint had been made against their wishes, and they believed the evidence was such as did not warrant his committal. But the magistrate immediately ordered Trellison to prison, and rebuked the young students for meddling with his official duties. The public feeling was very strong against Trellison, and scarcely any doubt remained, that on the next day he would be convicted of an aggravated assault, with intent to murder.

At this stage of the business, to the surprise of all, two young men, members of college, appeared and declared themselves the parties in fault. They stated, that having been in Roxbury[3] the preceding afternoon on a shooting excursion, they had taken supper at an inn on their way home, and after supper several persons came in, and the evening was occupied in card-playing and wine-drinking; the wine proved too strong for them, so much so as to make them wholly unconscious of the earthquake, the news of which surprised them, the next day. On their return home at a late hour, they saw a long distance behind them a light, which they supposed proceeded from the lantern of some members of college. They had now partially recovered from the effects of the wine, and on seeing this light, they resolved to play off a joke, and accordingly went into the neighboring woods and waited till the students came up; they then fired successively, aiming at the bushes a few rods in advance of the travellers. The guns were loaded with buckshot only, but they supposed the unsteadiness of their aim proceeded from the fumes of wine, and on hearing Strale remark that his hand was wounded, and seeing him by the light of the lantern hold it up to his companion, they feared the joke had been carried too far, and after waiting till the road was still, they went home.

This relation established the innocence of Trellison beyond all doubt, and very much to the annoyance of several officious individuals who had prejudged the case, and fully believed in his guilt. Walter and Lyford shared too in the awkwardness and confusion that followed. All they could do was to make a full apology, and express their deep regret at the course which had been taken. Trellison bowed haughtily, but in such a manner as to show that the offence would not readily be forgiven. The two young men who had made confession, were held to bail for subsequent examination, and the parties soon after dispersed.

CHAPTER SIXTH

A FEW DAYS after the adventure in the woods, Lyford obtained leave to visit his friends in Hadley. At that time such a journey was no small affair; and the road was so new, so little travelled, and the settlements on the way were so thinly scattered, that it required a good deal of preparation, and was usually performed on horseback. There were no inns on the road, except a small house in the settlement at Worcester, and a log cabin in the neighborhood of Brookfield, where food and lodging might be had.[1]

The journey was undertaken in company with a friend, and the ride of four days among the forests of New England was characterized by a variety of romantic and pleasing incidents. It was not without peril of life and limb, for the road was often precipitous, and though sometimes travelled in sleighs and wheel carriages, these conveyances were little adapted to its rugged surface, and afforded small comfort to their riders. The road was perfectly known to Lyford, and the scenery on the way was so picturesque and beautiful that he often paused in admiration on some of the cliffs over which his path led him, and gazed long and with lively interest at those wild and rugged features of nature which the labor of man has since softened into the calmer lineaments of pleasant meadows, flourishing gardens and cultivated fields.

The village of Hadley had been the residence of the venerated Gen. Goffe. Every incident in his grandfather's history, every spot which the illustrious exile loved, was dear to the memory of Lyford. In their early childhood, James and his sister were the solace of many a weary hour, and threw around the aged patriot the last gleams of sunshine which fell on his troubled career. Every one loved the old man; and the mandate of the royal Stuart and his bribe of gold[2] were of no force among the peaceful villagers, who well knew the veteran's retreat, and could never be persuaded, by promise or threat, to betray him. The sympathies of the community in which he lived were wholly on his side, and all those friendly offices which affection could suggest, or kindness confer, were liberally bestowed. But the tyrannical Charles was then in the zenith of his power, and the last days of Goffe were imbittered by the tidings of his constant and successful aggressions on the laws and liberties of England. Whatever were his errors in pronouncing judgment upon the only Stuart who commands the sympathy and affection of posterity, it is certain that Gen. Goffe deplored the necessity of such a sacrifice, and acted under a strong, but misguided sense of duty.[3] His name is yet held in honored and grateful remembrance; his ashes rest in a land where no kingly prerogative tramples with its iron foot on the sacred rights of man, and where the blessed vision that shone so brightly on his eye, is a living and glorious reality.

During Lyford's absence, his sister returned to Salem, and Walter applied himself with new vigor to his studies. Before

Mary left Boston, however, their mutual vows had been pledged, with the full consent of Walter's parents, whose reply to his earnest request was as kind and affectionate as he could desire. Strale had never requested Miss Graham to explain the circumstances of Trellison's long interview with her on his way home from Mr. Elliott's, but as she was aware of the difficulties which occurred at Cambridge on the next day, and of the singular and suspicious attitude in which Trellison's declaration had placed her, she now thought it proper to make Walter acquainted with all the facts in the case. It appeared that Mr. Trellison had long persisted in a class of attentions which were exceedingly annoying and disagreeable, and Miss Graham determined to accept his offer to accompany her home, with a view to put a final end to his importunities. On this occasion Trellison again renewed his request, that she would so far permit his attentions as to allow him the hope of a future union, declaring that his love was stronger than death, and that no conceivable suffering could be equal to that which must follow the abandonment of his hope. Miss Graham had long known the strength of his attachment, and in reply assured him that in many points he possessed her esteem and respect, but beyond that, she could give no response to his feelings, and begged he would cease his attentions, declaring once for all, that all hope and expectation on his part were entirely groundless, and must terminate, as her affections were already fixed upon another, and his duty to himself and to her required that he should no longer molest her with such attentions as she could never reciprocate.

The result of this interview accounted for the haggard and troubled appearance of Trellison on his return to Cambridge. It was a fatal blow to his hopes; it struck deeply at his pride, and aroused a train of reflections and purposes which, under various disguises, were so interwoven with the severity of his religious views, as to conceal from him in part their real turpitude. He could not forgive Strale for supplanting him, as he supposed, in Mary's love. He began to think Miss Graham herself was not the angelic being his fancy had pictured, and a feeling of bitterness against both soon passed over his mind, which he chose to indulge, as furnishing some antidote to the disappointment and shame which had nearly overwhelmed him.

It was now the clear sunshine of happiness with Walter. His long cherished object had been attained, and he looked forward with pride and pleasure to the day when he could call Miss Graham his own, and present her to his parents as the object of his warmest love.

Mary, too, was happy; but there was one blot in the beautiful picture she was contemplating. Strale was not decidedly religious. His principles were firm, his views of religion serious and respectful; but this was not sufficient or satisfactory. She was desirous most of all, that he might possess that inestimable pearl,[4] which he who obtains will never give up, and he who refuses to seek will never obtain. Her conversations with Walter on religious subjects were frequent and serious; and every day, while they were together, she had the happiness to find him more deeply interested, and more determined that his future well being should become a matter of personal concern and solicitude.

On the last evening before Mary left Boston, the conversation was more than usually interesting. The day had been clear and cold—there was little snow on the ground, but it presented a smooth surface of ice over which they found a pleasant walk on the borders of the forest which then occupied, in the wildness of its original growth, the present site of the Boston common.[5] The moonlight was falling among the trees, and was also reflected from the ice and snow, whose beautiful expanse was visible on the south. The subject of conversation was the character of New-England piety. Walter had serious objections to its general features, which he thought were unnatural and unwarranted by the scriptures. He objected to its harshness and severity, its alliance to bigotry and superstition, its restraint upon the buoyancy and cheerfulness of youth, and its rigid demands upon the time and attention of its professors.

'These, Mary,' said he, 'are difficulties which I cannot get over. Surely religion was never intended to strip the world of its beauty and clothe it in unnatural gloom. It must animate all our joyous sensibilities, and not suppress them—it must give us bright pictures of the future life, and not such as will cast shadows and gloom over the present.'

'Religion, Walter,' replied Mary, 'must strip the world of its false beauty, and present it in its true light. It must frown upon every sensibility, however joyous, which is sinful. It claims our supreme regard, and demands the first place in our pursuits, the first in our affections. The beauty and color of the richest wine are often heightened by the poisonous drug—shall we therefore press the chalice to our lips? Will you not agree with me that most of that which charms the youthful mind is false and illusive?'

'I have often found it so. But on the other hand, is there no excess in religious sensibility? Do not insanity and despair sometimes follow in the train of excited apprehensions of future wrath, and is not the imagination often terrified and distracted by groundless alarms?'

'This excess of sensibility is not peculiar to religious subjects. The intense application of the mind to any subject of absorbing interest will often destroy its balance, and unfit it for usefulness and happiness. How is it with the men of pleasure, of wealth, of talent and fame? Are they not overthrown sometimes by the excitement of their several vocations? And can religion, Walter, which is of all themes the most exciting, be always contemplated with such calmness as never to distract the mind?'

'It is not religion, dear Mary, that I object to; but to those distorted and unnatural shapes which it seems to wear in the community. Look now at the strange delusion which prevails at Salem. Under color of religion, several innocent persons have been imprisoned,[6] charged with crimes which they cannot commit if they would; and yet we are told the interests of true religion require their punishment.'

'These are the excrescences of religion,' replied Mary, 'not the thing itself. As to the witch stories, and the proceedings of the magistrates, there is folly enough about them; but I am quite sure no part of it is to be laid to religion. Superstition affects all minds more or less. It has a most powerful agency in the papal church, and is an important part of the machinery by which that evil system is supported. I believe there is less of it here than elsewhere; and yet if its elements are once in commotion, there is no absolute protection against its power. Not many years since several persons were punished in England for witchcraft, and it is unfortunate that the relations between the physical and mental states are not better understood. The ignorant and credulous too often mistake the disorders of their minds for the influence of mysterious spirits and malignant demons, and for want of a just discrimination, the most disastrous results will sometimes follow.'

'I am ashamed to confess, Mary, that my own experience goes to confirm the truth of your remarks. I am not wholly free from superstitious feelings. There have been times in my life when I was ready to start at the fall of a leaf, and have felt an undefinable and mysterious awe, for which I could trace no sufficient cause. I have been at times almost ready to sympathize with those who look at the blooming of a flower out of its season, or the sudden blighting of blossoms on the tree, as intimations of death or some other calamity. I remember a family of six brothers in Virginia, the youngest ten years of age, and all of them in sound and vigorous health. A number of peach trees in fine condition were growing in front of the house. They were very remarkable for the abundance and excellence of their fruit. Early in the spring before I left, those trees were observed to be full of blossoms, when suddenly, and without apparent cause, the bloom of three of them was blighted, and in a few weeks they died. Soon after I reached Boston I was informed by letter, that three of those brothers were successively seized with fever and died. Was not this, Mary, a shadow of things to come, a significant token of the desolation which so soon fell upon the family? Was it not at least remarkable in its circumstances?'

'Just now, Walter, you seemed to warn me against superstition, and then suggested a train of thought which could not fail to awaken it, if I had any. Indeed, Walter, I have no belief in its being a wonder, even as you state it. What is more common than for a peach tree to be full of blossoms, and then suddenly die? A worm at the root, a thousand blighting influences, are constantly at work to undermine its little life; and if the incident contains an impressive lesson, it does not warrant us in believing it the design of Providence to reveal thereby the deaths which soon after occurred.'

'You are not so credulous even, as I am,' said Walter, 'and I certainly am not so religious as you are. This would seem to prove there is no tendency in your religion to blend itself with superstition. It is therefore but reasonable that I should give up this point. Yet that superstition now reigns to an alarming degree in this very religious community is not to be denied. The singular antics and wild fancies[7] of those who are so strangely affected, will easily satisfy the multitude of the presence and power of evil spirits; and where shall we look for a remedy? Now, strange as it may seem to you, it is my belief, if public amusements were introduced, assemblies for dancing, and even theatrical exhibitions, these would do more to banish the delusion than any thing else. The truth is, I hear so many strange things, so well accredited from sources so respectable, that I half believe Satan has been let loose upon the community, and is moulding the opinions and conduct of men according to his own will.'

'The measures you propose, to drive him off,' said Mary, laughing, 'would rather induce him to stay. He is said to be very much at home in places where these amusements abound. Nevertheless, if I were sure he would be so well satisfied with the means you propose, as to let go his hold upon the fancies of the community, I think we might be gainers by the exchange. It would be substituting the lesser for the greater evil.'

'What surprises me most,' said Walter, 'is the ready credence which is given to those who say they are affected by witches. Judge Sewall, who is certainly a wise and cool tempered man, Gov. Stoughton, and other distinguished men, are firm believers in the reality of these affections; and there is even now an appeal to the Mosaic scriptures to punish witches with death. One of its commands, 'Thou shalt not suffer a witch to live,'[8] is quoted as a divine warrant for judicial proceedings; and such is the zeal manifested in the cause, I fear it will lead to the death of those individuals who are now in prison.'

'Well, Walter, whatever comes of it, do not, I pray you, impute it to religion. It has nothing to do with it. Some of the most pious in the land are doing all in their power to divert the public feeling into a different channel. There is Mr. Higginson, my own minister, of Salem,[9] venerable and beloved by all; Mr. Willard, here, Mr. Brattle and Mr. Leverett,[10] the latter your own tutor at Cambridge; all these, and many others, though to some extent believers in witchcraft, are entirely opposed to the interference of the law, and think the evil will soon cure itself. Let us trust in Providence that all will come right. And for you, dear Walter, I dread the thought that this mental epidemic should lead you to distrust for a moment the efficacy and power of the gospel. Believe it, Walter, for it is assuredly true: the gospel, received and trusted, is the best remedy for every mental and moral disorder.'

'It would be happy for me, dear Mary, could the same christian graces which adorn your character, shine forth in mine. I know that true piety towards God is my only safeguard from the ills of life, my only hope for the life to come. I believe in the great truths you profess. I long to experience their power in my own heart, and whatever sacrifice of the world it may cost, I hope through the mercy of a Redeemer, I shall be his willing and obedient disciple.'

The conversation closed as they reached the door of Mr. Hallam, with whose family Mary was to spend the last night of her stay in Boston.

It was not surprising that a superstition so unwarrantable should give to a mind like Strale's, false and unfavorable notions of religion. He imputed the delusion to what he thought the sternness and severity of the popular religious feeling, not considering that a simple analysis of the mind will develope a multitude of causes, upon which the imputation may far more justly rest. The conversation we have related tended very much to dispel this error, and in the painful scenes which were soon to be developed, he was enabled to distinguish with great accuracy between the religious principle and the wild and dreadful fanaticism with which it was attended.

CHAPTER SEVENTH

IT WAS NOW the latter end of February, 1692. The winter had been cold, and the ground since December had most of the time been covered with snow. Our young friend, James Lyford, we left in Hadley. He was spending a few weeks in the family of Mr. Temple, who in the days of General Goffe was his intimate friend, and by his generosity and personal society had contributed greatly to the quiet and happiness of the exiled patriot. James had spent his early youth in Hadley, and a thousand pleasant associations were connected with its natural scenery, and the localities and friends of his childhood. The little time allowed for his visit, passed rapidly away, and his engagements at college required his return early in March. He wished also to spend a few days in Worcester on his return, to see a friend who had just located in that new settlement. One of Mr. Temple's sons, named Henry, a lad of fourteen years of age, was permitted to accompany him.

The little fellow had heard much of Boston, and longed to see a place which contained so many objects to gratify curiosity. The notions of the peaceful villagers of Hadley, in those days, were confined very much to their own beautiful territories, and they never thought of visiting Boston except for purposes of business, and having supplied their wants, which were few and simple, they always gladly returned to their homes, and in the community of friendship and good will, together with the christian sympathy which pervaded their little settlement, they found a degree of contentment and happiness, to which wealth, fashion and luxury can never attain.

> 'Far from the madding crowd's ignoble strife,
>   Their sober wishes never learned to stray;
> Along the cool, sequestered vale of life,
>   They kept the noiseless tenor of their way.'[1]

But the youth of Hadley were not always satisfied with the quiet scenes of rural life. The fame of Boston, its high buildings, crowded market, the steeples and bells of the churches, the ships in the harbor, and its various objects of interest and attraction, possessed a charm which never invested their own blue hills and blooming forests. Boston at this time contained six thousand inhabitants, and was a beautiful town, covered with fine buildings, pleasant gardens, and streets ornamented by trees. Many of our young readers[2] will remember their feelings, when for the first time they came to visit this now splendid city, and will readily imagine those of young Temple, when the same prospect, though in miniature, was held out to his eye.

It required some special preparation for a journey to Boston, the distance being one hundred miles, and through a country but little travelled, and with only two inns on the road. The sleighing was now fine, and Lyford preferred this mode of conveyance, as they had several articles to carry, which could not be taken on horseback. Mr. Temple provided them with every thing necessary for themselves, and provender for the horse; they had also materials for producing fire, an axe, and a shovel, to be used in case of snow-drifts, besides the trunk which contained Lyford's clothes, and books; a rifle, with sufficient powder and ball, completed their arrangements for the journey.

Thus equipped, the two friends started on the twenty-sixth of February, and in the evening arrived at a little settlement, thirty miles from Hadley, where they passed the night. Leaving early the next morning, they hoped to reach Worcester in the evening, and they rode quietly most of the day, moving very slowly on account of the difficulties of the road, which was but slightly broken. The morning had been fine and clear, but towards noon the clouds came up, and the wind changed to northeast,—indicating one of those violent snow-storms which sometimes filled up the roads, and placed a long embargo on social intercourse. As the day declined, it began to snow, and James now urged his horse to his utmost speed, as they were far from any habitation, and there seemed no alternative, but either to get to Worcester, or perish in the woods. The snow was now falling thick and fast, with a high northeast wind directly in the faces of the travellers, and creating new obstacles to the already difficult road; the evening was at hand, and they were still ten miles from Worcester, and so violent was the storm, that it soon became evident they could not reach the settlement. In this dilemma, they hesitated for a moment, when James recollected a kind of shed he had seen on his way up, about a mile from their present position; and being assured that the only chance for their lives was in reaching that spot, they redoubled their efforts, James clearing the way with his shovel, and Henry leading the horse, the tempest meanwhile raging with the greatest violence.

The horse was now hardly able to keep his feet, having been jaded and exhausted by incessant toil, and they were still a quarter of a mile from the shed: at this moment they reached a high drift, which it seemed impossible to pass; and Henry, worn out with cold and fatigue, could no longer make the least effort. Lyford was now in the most alarming circumstances; he was himself greatly fatigued, and his strength could not much longer sustain him. He placed Henry in the sleigh, and covered him with blankets, while he returned to the snow-drift with his shovel, and in half an hour worked through. It was now dark, and the wind had fortunately blown the snow from the remainder of the road to the shed, which he reached at last, nearly overcome by anxiety and fatigue. It was well they found a resting-place there, for just before them an immense snow-drift reared its white and impassable barrier, which the strength of twenty men could not sufficiently reduce, and there was no circuit by which it could be avoided.

The shed under which our travellers were now resting, was built of logs, and wholly open in front; it faced the south, and its roof, composed of lighter wood, sloped nearly to the ground. It was built merely to feed horses on their way, and furnish a convenient spot, where travellers might rest for an hour. In one corner was a rough chimney, made of stones, but there was no furniture of any description, and little shelter from rain when the wind was south; but it seemed to our travellers, in their forlorn condition, like a home of safety and rest. They were yet unable to tell what might befall them, but their first duty of devout thanksgiving to a kind and protecting Providence was immediately and gratefully performed.

The storm had now increased to a furious tempest; the wind roared among the trees, and its wild and startling echoes sounded from the valleys and rocks. Sometimes they came in the loud tones of thunder, and then in the rapid sweep of the whirlwind; and vast clouds of snow were driven along the open spaces, and piled in huge heaps near the open front of the shed, affording some additional shelter to its inmates. But the place was at best a cold and comfortless lodging: there was no wood for a fire, and only the dim candle of the lantern to afford them light. In these circumstances, Lyford made the best possible arrangements for the night: the sleigh was placed in a corner, two large blankets were extended before it and fastened to a pole, which was secured to a low beam that ran across the shed, and by a rude frame-work supported its roof. This contrivance furnished a kind of enclosure, which kept out the snow, and afforded a partial shelter for the horse as well as themselves. The poor animal, thoroughly exhausted, on being loosed from the harness, immediately laid himself down, and was covered by a blanket, and protected as far as possible from the storm. Lyford prepared a bed in the sleigh, of such materials as he could collect, and after taking some refreshment they covered themselves and went quietly to rest.

When the morning appeared, the storm was wild and fierce as ever. An immense quantity of snow had fallen, the atmosphere was filled with its driving masses, and there seemed no prospect of a favorable change. Lyford dug his way a few steps from the shed, but it was vain to contend with the furious elements, and he was glad to retreat to his forlorn shelter. By the light of day he discovered a quantity of broken wood and branches of trees, which afforded them the relief of a fire; and this was the more necessary, as the air was now excessively cold. A survey of their supplies followed, by which it appeared their corn and provisions were sufficient, with economy, for eight or ten days; the horse, however, it was necessary to keep on very short allowance, as there was little prospect that they could proceed on their journey for ten days at least.

On the third day the storm abated, and in the afternoon the sun came forth in his glory. Lyford succeeded in digging his way to a neighboring tree, and ascended to its topmost branches, where he beheld a vast and trackless expanse of snow, which had spread over hill and valley to an average depth of nearly three feet, but which in many places was piled like mountains, and seemed to defy all the power of man to break down its barriers and force a passage.

As Lyford descended from the tree, he saw a dark object on the snow, about a quarter of a mile distant, and in the direction of what appeared to be the road. It first seemed like the trunk of a tree, which had been burned to a coal, yet he soon perceived it had a slow motion towards him. His curiosity was strongly excited, and he gazed with increasing interest, until the outlines of a human figure were distinctly visible, as it dragged its slow pace through the heavy snow-drifts towards Lyford. In about an hour from the time he was discovered, Pompey—for it was no other than he—stood before Lyford, who was extremely perplexed and surprised at his sudden appearance.

'Be this you, Massa James?' said Pompey. 'How came you up in dis tree, and among dese snow banks?'

'It will be time enough to ask these questions when I get out. But what brings you here, Pompey?'

'Come to find you, Massa. Went to Wooster first, but no Massa Lyford there—so I came all the way here. Will you tell me, Massa, where I get something to eat?'

'All in good time. But where did you stay last night, Pompey?—you could hardly walk a mile a day through such snow-drifts as these.'

'Staid in the trunk of a tree, Massa, these two nights, and glad to get there,—snow-storm drove me in. I look out to-day, and saw a man climb a tree. I thought if Pompey get to that man, he may find something better than snow to eat.'

'Hard fare, Pompey; how do you like this blessed land now?'

'Nothing but trouble in it, Massa James; kicks, prisons, and snow-storms. No such things in Virginny. Hope Massa Walter send me back before de debils carry me off. Boston and Salem full of debils as dey can hold; de women full of debils, too, and de men running as if de debils were after them. Here's a letter for you, Massa Lyford.'

James took Pompey to the shed, where the poor negro obtained some food, and was soon in a condition to give some further account of himself. The letter he brought was from Strale, in which he requested Lyford to return without delay. He stated that universal distrust prevailed, and that consternation and dismay extended to every circle; the regular studies at college were interrupted, accusations for witchcraft were coming in from every quarter, and it was fully believed the reign of Satan had commenced. For himself, he held the popular notions in utter contempt; but it was foolish and dangerous to oppose them openly, and he begged that Lyford would not tarry at Worcester, but return at once, as his counsel and assistance might be necessary; and as no one was safe, it was better for him to be at home, where such measures might be adopted, as the course of events should require.

Walter had despatched this letter to Worcester, in the expectation that Lyford was there; but the faithful negro, finding he had not arrived, pushed on towards Hadley, until driven by the snow-storm into such shelter as he could find, when he fortunately discovered Lyford in the manner we have related.

It was impossible to leave the shed with any hope of making progress through the snow; the travellers were therefore compelled to wait for a change of weather. They succeeded in procuring wood enough in the neighborhood to keep up their fire, and by good management they were tolerably comfortable for a few days. During this time, the solitary waste was cheered by no voice or track of man; all was silent, save that now and then the loud report of Lyford's rifle, aimed at some passing wild-fowl, sent its echoes among the trees: but on the sixth day a gentle south wind sprung up, which was soon followed by a cloudy sky, and in the evening torrents of rain began to fall, which deluged the country like a flood. It continued all the next day, and it was with great difficulty a dry spot could be preserved in the shed. In the evening it cleared up; the wind suddenly changed to northwest, and became extremely cold. The next day, being the eighth from the time they first entered the shed, the travellers were again on their way over a smooth surface of snow and ice; and in two hours the little cluster of houses at the settlement, with its white church spire, greeted their eyes, and gave them promise of refreshment and rest.[3]

Such adventures as these were very common among the pioneers of New England. Her vigorous and hardy population,

despising the rigor of the climate, penetrated her deepest re-
cesses, planted themselves in the midst of her forests, and there,
rich in contentment, in honest industry and vigorous health, and
above all in the unfettered exercise of the rights of conscience,
they fulfilled their work on earth, and calmly and peacefully descended to their graves. Other generations like themselves have
filled the land; the welcome of hospitality, the house of God, the
family altar, the blessed Bible, and the thousand endearments
of home and friends,—these, all these, and unnumbered other
blessings, have been conferred upon New England by her primitive inhabitants, and are at once the monuments of their fidelity, and the pledges that if the sons walk in the footsteps of the
fathers,[4] she will continue to advance in national eminence and
glory.

CHAPTER EIGHTH

THE DEMON OF superstition was now abroad in New England. The unaccountable delusion of witchcraft so pervaded the public mind, that suspicions and jealousies were engendered among the nearest friends; perplexity and astonishment were visible in every countenance. So strange were the movements of those who were supposed to be affected by demons, and such the confessions of reputed witches, that men of sober judgment and highly gifted minds were involved in the general belief, and united in the execration of those who were believed to be confederate with Satan and his emissaries. Neither age nor rank were exempted from suspicion, and those who were charged with practicing witchcraft upon almost any testimony, were arrested and committed to prison. Many deserted their homes and went into other parts of the country; days of fasting and prayer were multiplied; parts of the Bible were hung around the neck, as a defence against the power of the devil; and a constant dread of the black book[1] which was supposed to be in circulation among the witches, and was said to contain the terms of treaty with

Satan, kept the minds of the credulous in constant distress and anxiety.

This delusion, it is well known, prevailed mostly in Salem and its vicinity. To the disturbed fancies of the populace, the very air was peopled with demons, and Satan, loosed from his chains, was tormenting men before their time. A few persons withstood the delusion, but it was at the peril of their lives, if they attempted open opposition: such was the popular frenzy that, if any question were raised as to the reality of these unseen agencies, it was considered a fair case for prosecution, and the bold innovator was in constant peril of reputation and life. Still there were some who had the courage to remonstrate, and who employed every art of persuasion and influence to stay the ruin which they saw was coming on the land. They also favored the escape of many who were accused; and, though believers themselves, to a certain extent, in this kind of Satanic influence, they always opposed those measures of cruelty and shame, in which the fatal tragedy was finally closed.

Among these benevolent and excellent men, the names of Willard of Boston, Brattle of Cambridge and Higginson of Salem are most conspicuous. These gentlemen refused all part in the witch prosecutions, and earnestly protested against bringing the crime of witchcraft before the civil tribunals, alleging that the individuals charged with this sin were in the hands of God, who alone had a right to punish them, and that the liability to mistake in the nature of the evidence, and the want of a just discrimination, on a subject so mysterious, entirely disqualified the courts to act upon such cases. Their efforts, however, were in vain; yet it may be reasonably believed that, to some extent, they were able to modify and soften the proceedings of the courts, though it was impossible to control or suppress them.

Lyford started for Boston about the tenth of March, spending but a single day at Worcester. The people at this settlement were astonished at the tidings which reached them from Boston and Salem; but they were fortunate enough to escape the mania, and, though disposed to the same general belief, they viewed the cases of such as were accused in a much more calm and benevolent light, and were disposed to regard them as subjects of pity and prayer rather than as outcasts from God and man. But as Lyford approached Boston, he discovered among the people a bitter hatred of the supposed witches, and a belief that no service could be more pleasing to God than to destroy them utterly from the land. He saw at once the terrible engine of power, which designing men might seize to punish private wrongs, and push their projects of revenge for real or supposed injuries. He knew the self-blinding power of the human mind, and how readily its dark purposes assume the form of religious duties and wear the counterfeit of the heavenly graces. And it was this view that filled him with apprehensions and forebodings, which neither conscious rectitude nor the power of reason could allay.

It was the first object of Lyford, after seeing Strale, to visit his sister at Salem; but as he could give no satisfactory reason for his journey, without disclosing his relation to Mary, the government of the college refused his request, and his long absence in the winter was assigned as the cause. In this dilemma, it was determined that Walter, to whom this objection did not apply, should visit Salem and ascertain the true state of things, and the danger, if any, to which Mary might be exposed. The engagement of the parties was now publicly known, and Walter's request was immediately granted.

On his arrival at Salem, which was about the latter part of March, he found such a state of consternation and terror as could scarcely be described. Witches were every where. They would flit through the streets after sunset; and at an early hour in the evening, demons, with long tails and cloven feet, were stalking about, partly concealed in mists and shadows, but taking care to show enough of their origin to keep the good people of Salem within doors after dark, and thus they had the whole promenade to themselves. Some of the old ladies averred that they were visible in the day time, and that one of them was perched in Mr. Higginson's pulpit on a Sabbath afternoon and kept the place till the good man opened the Bible and read the passage about resisting the devil, when he suddenly decamped, leaving behind him a long train of fire, and filling the church with the fumes of sulphur. Mr. Higginson did not, however, appear conscious of the victory he had attained; for, when told of it the next day, he remarked, that he never supposed such extraordinary power in any one passage of the Bible; but since the testimony was so clear, he hoped they now possessed the means of expelling all the evil spirits in Salem, and he prayed that his people would not fail to use these weapons, as they were certainly lawful, and their own observation had shown them to be successful.

Mary Graham had resided, for several years, in the family of Mr. Ellerson. This gentleman was of course acquainted with all the circumstances of her history, and had manifested towards her the utmost kindness and friendship. In fact, no one, at all acquainted with Miss Graham, could fail to esteem and admire her character. It had been the special care of Mrs. Ellerson to instruct her in all the pleasing accomplishments of genteel life, and at the same time, to restrain her from those amusements and follies, which dissipate the mind and unfit it for religious contemplation and duty; she therefore gave, as much as possible, a serious complexion to her studies and seasons of social enjoyment. The pupil well repaid the care of the teacher, and, at the age of eighteen, beautiful, accomplished and beloved by all, she entered the best circles, and we have already had some glimpses of the virtues which adorned her character. Mr. and Mrs. Ellerson had been consulted in every stage of her relations to Strale, and the affair was not concluded without their entire concurrence and approval. Walter was of course a welcome visiter at their house, whenever he had opportunity and leave of absence from college. But these seasons were necessarily very infrequent, as the college discipline allowed little time for recreation, and required a strict attention to the regular studies.

The circumstances in which Walter now found his friends, were altogether new and peculiar. A gloom was spread over the town, which was relieved by no cheerful meetings of friends, no lively airs of music, nor even the busy hum of trade. The streets of the village were silent as the fields that surrounded them, and the necessary offices of kindred and friendship were imbittered by suspicion, and discharged with indifference and coldness. The common ties of relationship and affection were nearly dissolved, and piety itself was forced into unnatural relations with credulity and superstition.

About twenty persons were now in prison, awaiting their trial for practicing witchcraft; others were daily suspected and arrested; and there was scarcely an individual in Salem, who was not more or less under the influence of this delusion. Mr. and

Mrs. Ellerson were among the most incredulous; yet facts and statements were daily going the rounds, which were so well supported, and the reality of this mystical influence was so generally believed, that persons as reflecting and considerate even as they were, did not escape the incipient stages of the public malady.

The hour for tea had nearly arrived, when Walter entered the parlor of Mr. Ellerson. Mary was not at home, having engaged to pass the afternoon and evening with the Misses Higginson. Mr. and Mrs. Ellerson were also absent, and Walter, after having spent an hour with Mary and her companions, and engaged to return for her in the evening, went back to await the arrival of his friends, the Ellersons. They returned about seven o'clock, and the conversation was very soon directed to the prevailing topic of the day.

'You have a strange atmosphere in Salem,' said Walter; 'every thing looks unnatural and melancholy; I hope the witches have kept away from your house, Mr. Ellerson?'

'They would not find very pleasant quarters here, Walter; but as all the other houses in town are full, they may for want of better accommodations force their way in. Their reception might be somewhat cold, but I am told they are not very scrupulous where they once get possession.'

'It is a singular business,' replied Walter; 'but the more I think of it, the stronger is my conviction that it is all a fatal delusion, foolish, wonderful, and wicked. I have no patience with such follies. I have heard to-day stranger things than I ever read in the tales of the fairies, the legends of Bagdad, or the whole system of pagan fables.'[2]

'You are always rash, Walter. You must look at the evidence in favor of any alleged fact, however strange, before you decide against its truth. Have you seen any who profess to be troubled by witches?'

'I have not,' said Walter; 'but that makes no difference; the stories are incredible. There is no such influence at the present day, if there ever was.'

'I am going this evening, Walter,' said Mr. Ellerson, 'to see for myself. There is a reputed witch, and a person said to be afflicted by her, who reside about half a mile from us. I shall be glad if you will go with me.'

'Nothing will please me better,' said Walter. 'I have often felt the influence of Satan, but have never seen him, and if he now makes his appearance in this gross, terrestrial atmosphere, I would like to know if my senses can discern him. I think we shall see he has many ways of making fools of even sober and considerate men.'

In a short time they set off, and a walk of ten minutes among the pleasant gardens and cottages of Salem, brought them to a house, where a crowd of people had gathered to witness the visible power of devils over men. As they entered the room, a female dressed in the rustic fashion of the country, was seated in a chair before them. She was pale and silent, but there was a wildness in her appearance, and a fierce expression in her eye, which indicated that strange elements were at work, suppressed for the time, but liable to act at any moment with fearful energy. A supposed witch was presently conducted into the room. She was an old lady, of tottering gait, and apparently in very feeble health, but perfectly self-possessed and quiet. At sight of her, the afflicted person sprang into the air, and uttering the wildest cries, she raved about the room, and was hardly restrained by the force of two men from escaping to the street. In a moment more, she sat down with comparative tranquillity; but again her frame was agitated, and she was suddenly lifted with no visible effort, and seemed for a moment suspended in the air; then falling on the floor, she was quiet a little while, when she gradually assumed a sitting posture, and began to reason with some master demon, and called upon the witch to cease her torment.

'I have nothing to do with your torment,' said the old lady.

'Then it is Satan that does it, by your means,' said the girl.

'I have nothing to do with Satan, and know not what your torments are,' was the reply.

'That is the way Satan blinds you. When you are gone, I have no suffering.'

'You have greatly wronged me,' replied the lady; 'and on this account I have no doubt my presence is painful to you. I hope God will forgive you, and restore that reason, which in his inscrutable wisdom he has taken away.'

The old lady was now removed from the room, when the afflicted person relapsed into a state of quiet, which was of course attributed to the absence of the exciting cause.

'This is a juggler's game, Mr. Ellerson,' said Walter; 'that person accused is no more a witch than I am. If it be not an intended cheat, it is a diseased mind, or a nervous irritability, which has been trained into a system, and acts with some regularity. These people are some of them knaves, and most of the remainder are fools; the reputed witch is the only one in her right mind.'

'I cannot decide so readily as you. There is some evidence in the Scriptures of the reality of visible, Satanic influence, but I am inclined to believe there has been little, if any of it, since the Christian era; but how that female preserves her stationary posture in the air, with no visible support, I cannot imagine. If you, Walter, are wise on this point, I wish you would enlighten me.'

'There is some mystery in it,' said Strale, 'but so there is in every thing. To believe such follies we must renounce common sense, and I had almost said a belief in a beneficent Providence. I have seen persons poised on the fingers of others, in such a manner as to be apparently unaffected by gravitation; the cause, no one explains; but if such cases are scrutinized, it will doubtless be found they are perfectly consistent with natural laws. Think you, Mr. Ellerson, it is possible that the devil has such power on earth?'

'He is the prince of the power of the air,' replied Mr. Ellerson. 'We know that in the time of Christ, he did exercise power over the bodies and minds of men, and may it not be impious in us to deny that he has such influence now, though it may be in less degree?'

'I would not be impious or irreverent on this or any other subject,' rejoined Walter; 'yet there are so many natural causes, which may account for these things, that I am very slow to attribute them to the agency of Satan. I believe a limited power over man is possessed by the arch apostate, but it seems to me the period of its physical developement was confined to the early ages of the Christian church, just as the age of miracles was measured and limited by the necessities of the church. I doubt not he retains power to tempt men. I have felt it myself, alas! too often; but, Mr. Ellerson, since I have known Mary, she has led me to a brighter path of contemplation and hope. I would be no visionary theorist; I would be an humble, serious, every-day Christian.'

'Such, dear Walter, I would have you to be. Such, indeed, I trust you are,' replied Mr. Ellerson. 'True piety enlightens as well as purifies; and let not, I pray you, this mysterious delusion, for such I must regard it, disturb your faith in that Gospel, which must be your only hope, for time and eternity. What will be the issue of these troubles, no one can tell. A dark cloud has come over the land; when it shall pass away is known only to Him, to whom darkness and the day are alike.'

They had now reached Mr. Ellerson's dwelling. It was a beautiful habitation, and the moon was shining brightly over the garden and a neighboring grove, and falling in placid radiance on a little stream which glided through the field. That spot is now covered by mansions of opulence and comparative grandeur; but the romance of the scene has passed away, the white fence of the garden is broken down; the bed of the stream is covered by the green earth, and the moonbeams shine over the works of taste and art; but not with the simplicity and grace in which they danced upon the forest oak and the tangled grove.

Walter remained a few days at Salem, and notwithstanding the state of things around him, it was one of the happiest periods of his life: another and a sweeter illusion occupied his mind; the bright pictures of coming days, undefaced by a single visible stain, passed in rapid succession before his charmed imagination; the hopes of future years gathered in beautiful groups on his eye, while he felt that the lovely object, around which these visions were glittering, would soon be his own.

During this brief period, the conversation of the two friends was devoted mainly to the subject of religion. The holy influences of the Gospel had found their way to the mind and heart of Strale. He saw in a new light the wonderful scheme of redemption; he admired and adored the grace which had made him a partaker of its blessings, and he resolved that his whole future life should illustrate its excellence and glory.

We need not speak of the joy that glowed in the heart of Mary, as she beheld and admired the change. Her cup of worldly happiness was full to overflowing; she looked even upon the distracted community around her in a calm reliance on Him who controls the tempest and stills its rage; but she saw not the dark cloud that was even then gathering in her sky; she heard not the dashing of those waves, which were soon to ingulf her dearest hopes. The song of the sirens[3] was too sweet to be hushed by the distant thunder, and her unconscious feet were already treading on the fatal shore.

CHAPTER NINTH

NOTHING IS MORE essential to a well-ordered civil government, than a well-balanced public mind; for want of this, in different ages, laws have been framed and penalties executed in cases which go beyond the reach of human investigation, and relate to subjects of which we can form only faint and obscure conceptions, and consequently all the evidence touching such cases is more or less to be distrusted.

At the period we are now contemplating, the connection between the spiritual world and the physical being of man was supposed to be developed in an extraordinary degree. It was believed the boundaries between the material and invisible states were more clearly defined, and that strange and startling intercourse was held by mysterious agents, on these border territories. It was indeed no novelty in those days for the civil courts to claim jurisdiction over the rambling vagaries of the mind, and so far as any law affecting the social or civil compact was plainly violated, it was certainly within their office to punish the offence; but the courts travelled out of their way, and, invading the natural rights of man, they entered a field of inquiry, whose dim and uncertain forms could never be reduced to facts, or supply materials of evidence, on which a sober mind could rely. Of this nature was the court organized by Sir William Phips,[1] for the trial and punishment of witches. It had no legitimate character, and the functions it assumed were entirely beyond the rights of any earthly tribunal. Nevertheless, its authority was acknowledged, and its stern and dreadful mandates were obeyed as promptly as they were issued. The influence of this court, by giving judicial sanction to the extravagances of the times, tended very much to strengthen and prolong the delusion, and the remarkable infatuation of the judges overcame the plain common sense of the jury, which but for their influence would soon have checked the mania, and restored the public mind to calmness and reason.

We have before remarked, that Mr. Willard, the minister of the South Church, was strongly opposed to the proceedings of the courts. This was the more remarkable from the fact, that the chief justice and two of the judges were members of his church. Mr. Willard admitted the possibility of Satanic influence, but he denied that it was visible in any such form as to warrant judicial interference. He remonstrated with great earnestness against the general movements, and there is no doubt he suffered so much reproach on this account, that his remarkable talents and exemplary piety could scarcely sustain him. It is certain also, that he was accused of practicing witchcraft, and though the complaint was rejected by the court, there were not wanting those who believed him confederate with Satan, and a direct agent in promoting his designs upon the people of New England. There were some, however, who took Mr. Willard's ground, and boldly maintained that the court was illegal, and could not in any sense take cognizance of such matters. We have already mentioned Thomas

Brattle and John Leverett, tutors of Harvard College; and there is good reason to believe President Mather was of the same opinion, and attempted to restrain the popular feeling; but no one was more bold than Robert Calef, an eminent merchant of Boston,[2] whose views on the subject were as sound and discriminating as those of any man of that age. No individual did more to dispel the delusion, and the records he has left behind have reared an imperishable monument to his courage, fidelity, and success.

Miss Graham had accepted an invitation from her friend Miss Elliott, to spend the last two weeks of May in Boston. An intimate and endeared friendship now existed between these two young ladies. It was greatly promoted by Lyford, who had carefully studied the character of his sister's friend, and there was no one in his judgment who surpassed Miss Elliott in moral excellence, as well as mental accomplishments. Every attention had been bestowed upon her education; and though her manners and appearance were more formal and stately than comported with the simplicity of the times, yet she universally secured the respect and good-will of all classes in society.

It was grateful to Mary's feelings to retire for a while from the painful scenes she was every day compelled to witness at home. Her health and spirits were sinking under the strange excitement which pervaded the community at Salem and its neighborhood, and the change she sought was now absolutely necessary. The two friends were entirely agreed in matters of religious faith, and their intercourse with the world was regulated by a scrupulous regard to Christian decorum and example. The fashionable society of Boston was at that time professedly religious; the outward forms of devotion were generally and greatly respected; yet a powerful current of worldly influence was visible, and the clergymen of those days complained that the vital power of the Gospel was far too little manifested, in the lives and conversation of its professors.

On Miss Graham's arrival at Boston, she was visited by all her friends; but the usual routine of social parties was now nearly suspended. The painful suspicions and jealousies that were abroad had interrupted the peace of families, and extensive divisions in the churches and in general society were disturbing the public harmony, and shaking the foundations of social confidence in a most alarming degree. Still the state of things was far better than in Salem; and though the popular feeling even in Boston went along with the belief in supernatural agencies, yet there was enough of common sense remaining to oppose a formidable barrier to the action of courts and judges in the business. This conservative influence prevailed most in the first and third churches;[3] but in the congregation of Cotton Mather,[4] which was very large, there was scarcely a dissenting voice from the general belief, and the Sabbath day exercises at the North Church were almost exclusively governed by the impressions of an invisible world; and the church itself was regarded as the grand post of observation, from which the march and countermarch of Satan's ranks were discerned, while he moved at their head, enlisting recruits for his new kingdom, about to be established.

On the last week in May,[5] a day of fasting and prayer had been solemnly observed in reference to the prevailing calamities. The point of Satan's visible agency was now scarcely disputed, and those who doubted or disbelieved were in too much personal danger to make any public protest against the prevalent doctrines; yet it was scarcely possible for one who entertained such views as Walter to avoid an occasional sarcasm;

and Miss Graham herself was disposed to treat the subject with lightness, in the hope that its folly might in this way be more readily seen. The high standing they occupied was to some extent security from danger. But, on the other hand, there was a feeling of envy and jealousy towards the unsuspecting maiden, which soon involved her in suspicions; and Miss Hallam, who regarded Walter's attachment to Mary with extreme displeasure, availed herself of the general distrust to produce unfavorable impressions wherever her influence extended.

In this state of things the last Sabbath in May arrived. The religious exercises of the week had prepared the people to expect that their ministers would follow up the subject, and give such views of the whole case as comported with their own convictions, and the teachings of Scripture. The day was singularly beautiful; the freshness of its early dawning, and the summer breezes, that were diffusing life and joyousness around, were expressive of a mild and beneficent Providence; but Nature in her calm and delightful aspect, was all unconscious of the dark figures and mysterious demons, that were thronging the imaginations of men; her morning hymn was ascending in grateful chorus from forest, valley, and stream; but she was no longer the handmaid of devotion, for man refused to mingle in her silent or audible aspirations, or in any sense, to bend the knee at her shrine.

At ten o'clock, the bells rang for public worship, and the streets, which till then had been silent as the desert, were now thronged with multitudes on their way to the house of God. Sadness and sorrow were visible in every countenance. The early flowers of spring, the narcissus, the violet, and the snowdrop, which were wont to adorn the dresses, or fringe the hair of the young and beautiful, were utterly neglected, and the silent processions moved along the streets to their respective places of worship, as if they were following the dead to their burial. Even the church bells, which sent their cheerful melodies among the valleys and rocks, now seemed to toll upon the ear, the funeral dirge of all that was bright and happy in the land; the merry laugh of childhood, the clear sunshine of the brow of youth, and the serene tranquillity of maturer years, were suppressed and clouded by an unseen yet terrible influence, before whose mysteries Reason was overthrown, and Religion herself was staggered.

Miss Elliott and Mary, accompanied by their brothers and Strale, left home at the usual time for public worship. As they passed along on their way to the South Church, they were deeply impressed with the state of feeling so obvious around them; to see their fellow beings enslaved by a superstition so unnatural and absurd, to be unable to break the fatal spell which had fallen upon nearly all, and to mark in the dim future those undefined yet assuredly fatal consequences, of whose nature and extent the worst apprehensions might be indulged, filled their minds with anxiety and sorrow. But they endeavored to turn from these sad meditations to the hopes and consolations of the Gospel they loved, and which they firmly believed would deliver the mind from its debasing thraldom, and give to its emancipated powers 'the glorious liberty of the sons of God.'[6]

The South Church occupied the ground on which the present edifice stands, and its site was then called 'the Green.' It was constructed of cedar, and for those times it was an imposing and beautiful edifice; its tall spire, rising from the midst of a grove of buttonwood trees, and far above all surrounding objects, was gazed at with an interest and reverence which in these days is not often bestowed on those significant emblems which point upward to a 'house not made with hands, eternal in the heavens.'[7]

The pulpit was located, as now, in the northeast side of the building, and directly in front was a row of seats designed for and occupied by the elders. A small enclosure, still further in front, and facing the congregation, was occupied by the deacons, and before them was a platform, on which the leader of the music stood and conducted the psalmody, in which all who were able to sing, and some who were not, were in the habit of uniting.

On the present occasion, the service was commenced as usual by a prayer occupying about ten minutes, and followed by a psalm from the New-England version then in use,[8] which was first read by Mr. Willard, and then given out by the ruling elder, line by line, to the congregation. The selection for the morning was the fifty-first psalm, and its penitential character was strikingly adapted to the time and circumstances of their worship. Many a charming voice united in the simple melody, and many a contrite heart mingled its confessions and prayers, in the true spirit of devotion, with those of the pious psalmist.

As we wish to bring into view the principal features of Sabbath-day worship in those times, we give the following version of the psalm, in the words in which it was sung:

> 'HAVE mercy upon me, oh God!
>   According to thy grace;
> According to thy mercies great,
>   My trespasses deface.

'Oh! wash me throughly from my guilt,
>   And from my sin, me clear;
For I my trespass know, my sins
>   Before thee still appear.

'Of joy and gladness, make thou me
>   To hear again the voice;
That so the bones, which thou hast broke,
>   May cheerfully rejoice.

'From the beholding of my sin
>   Hide thou away thy face;
Likewise, all mine iniquities,
>   Oh! do thou clean deface.'[9]

The musical critic may sneer at the peculiar metre and simple versification, but it is probable the true design of sacred music was far more readily attained in those days and in this homely garb, than it can be by the high pretensions and meretricious ornaments of its modern masters.

The position of Mr. Willard was one of painful embarrassment. He had publicly declared his dissent from the prevalent opinions, and in this advanced stage of the popular delusion, when its early opposers were every day falling into the ranks of its believers, it required no small share of moral courage to maintain his ground. It was expected he would now make known his opinions without reserve, and that these opinions would appear greatly modified, if not totally changed. In this expectation, the church was thronged by multitudes who were anxious to quote his name and authority in support of the wild theories, which were now so generally adopted and believed.

The prayer which followed the music was distinguished for its fervency and pathos, and as the pastor carried up the desires of the congregation in his own affecting and impressive language, the fixed and solemn attention of the audience, indicated that it was no formal service, but one in which all the powers of the soul were deeply absorbed. At the close of the prayer, another psalm was sung, in the following words:

> 'THOU hid'st in wrath and us pursuest,
>   Thou slay'st and dost not rue;
> Thou so with clouds dost hide thyself,
>   Our prayer cannot pass through.
>
> 'Fear and a snare is come on us,
>   Waste and destruction;
> For my folks' daughters, now mine eyes
>   Run water rivers down.
>
> 'Come thou into thy chambers, shut
>   Thy doors about thee fast;
> Hide thou awhile, my people,
>   Awhile, till wrath be past.
>
> 'Lo! from his place God comes again
>   The world for sin to smite;
> Earth will her blood reveal—her slain—
>   Earth will bring all to light.'[10]

The text was then announced, and was at once indicative of the sentiments and designs of the preacher. It was the first verse of the fourth chapter of John's Epistle: 'Beloved, believe not every spirit, but try the spirits whether they be of God.'[11]

The preacher assumed as an undoubted fact, fully warranted by the Scriptures, that spiritual agencies for good and ill were constantly at work among men, but it was so difficult to define their nature, their peculiar offices, and the extent of their power, that it was our wisdom to avoid all speculation, except so far as was necessary to guard against practical error.

It was now a popular theory, that evil spirits assumed visible forms, and were permitted to make compacts or treaties with such as were pleased with their terms and conditions. This doctrine he denounced as in the highest degree absurd and dangerous, declaring it was a delusion fraught with the worst consequences, that the kind of evidence by which this theory was supported was totally unwarranted, and could not for a moment be trusted by a sound and discriminating mind.

He then proceeded to analyze the mind, its nature, its liability to mistake, its unsuspected deceits, its love of fable and delight in the marvellous and supernatural. He pointed out the frequent errors of the imagination; that it changes material substances, and creates in air, on earth, and in the ocean, innumerable shapes, which it clothes in beauty or gloom, according to the light in which these objects are contemplated. He then described its effects on the physical system, producing nervous agitation, fancied maladies, and strange distortions of the countenance, which it falsely attributes to unnatural and unreal causes.

Such being the character of the mind, it was impossible in the nature of the case to discriminate so accurately between its own actings and those of spiritual agents, as to measure the criminality of persons charged with the practice of witchcraft, or warrant the interference of the civil law. It often happens that a state of mind, supposed to be in the highest degree criminal, is the result of insanity and disease, and calls for sympathy and relief, instead of reproach and punishment; and in conclusion he declared his full conviction, that a lying spirit, like that of the prophets of Ahab,[12] was now abroad in the land, and in the fulness of his grief over the public calamities, he entreated and charged his people to try the spirits, to criticise severely every ground of accusation; for among the devices of Satan, none were more common than deception and fraud, and it was not impossible for him to persuade even the pious to believe a lie, for he was a liar from the beginning, and himself the father of lies.

Such a sermon and at such a time, could not fail to produce a strong excitement. As the congregation retired from the house, signs of displeasure were manifest on every side. The high reverence in which the character of Mr. Willard had been held, could scarcely restrain the general feeling of anger; but there were some who deeply sympathized with their minister, and felt that this noble testimony against the prevailing delusion, was as imperiously demanded, as it was faithfully and fearlessly given.

CHAPTER TENTH

'IT IS GOOD to see a little light in these dark days,' said Lyford,[1] addressing Miss Elliott on their return from church. 'Mr. Willard has acted the hero and the christian.'

'He has indeed,' said Margaret; 'I hope his counsels will be regarded; for I am confident he has given them at the risk of his life.'

'I never before heard a sermon,' said Lyford, 'which contained so much sound mental philosophy. If feeling and fanaticism condemn it, reason and common sense will approve. But he who has most of the former, and least of the latter, is counted the wisest man in these days.'

'Yet these are times,' said Margaret, 'in which the truly wise man may add vastly to his stock of wisdom. It is interesting after all to trace the windings and workings of this fanaticism, especially when it acts upon such minds as Cotton Mather's. This man is a perfect paradox to me. His mind is original and bold, yet his language is often so puerile as to disgrace his intellect. His manners and conversation are pleasing and often fascinating; he is beyond all his compeers in industry and intelligence, yet his

pedantry and superstition are intolerable. I have a great desire
to hear him preach this afternoon. Miss Graham also wishes to
go; and as the occasion is so remarkable, I think we shall be
justified in leaving our own church. If you and Mr. Strale will
accompany us, your curiosity at least will be gratified, and we
hope some greater good may be the result.'

Walter and Lyford readily consented, and when the interval of
public worship had elapsed, the party went to the North Church,
where the services commenced at two o'clock. An immense
congregation had assembled, for it was understood Mr. Mather
would defend the popular theories, and on such an occasion no
one could be listened to with more interest and attention. After
the preliminary exercises by Dr. Mather, which were exceedingly interesting, and a psalm of nearly the same character as
those sung at the South Church in the morning, the text was
announced by Cotton Mather from Isaiah xxviii, 15:[2] 'For your
covenant with death shall be disannulled, and your agreement
with hell shall not stand. When the overflowing scourge shall
pass by, ye shall be trodden down by it.'

The great object of this discourse was to support the position
that Satan has confederates among men, and that some of these
individuals are parties to a covenant or agreement, in virtue of
which they are regularly enlisted in his service, and empowered
to act in his behalf.

The nature and provisions of this contract, he alleged, were
in general uniform, though in some cases slight variations were
made, and now and then special powers were conferred. The confessions of witches, and the concurring testimony of the Bible,
furnished an amount of proof on this subject, which, however
remarkable and opposed to the usual course of events, could

not be rejected without incurring the displeasure of God, and subjecting the land to still greater encroachments from the powers of darkness. The providence of God had unfolded a variety of facts from which we were enabled to state the general terms and conditions on which the confederacy was founded, and he felt it due to the occasion and to his people to make known its principal features, in the belief that it might induce his hearers to watch the first approaches of Satan, and shun every possible temptation.

To the mind, in its common apprehensions, he said the influence of Satan was only perceived in the general forms of temptation and suggestion; but in proportion as it yielded its consent to sin, in these days of Satan's peculiar power, its perceptions of the invisible world became enlarged and distinct, and the advantages and pleasure of sin were greatly magnified, while its dreadful consequences were thrown entirely in the back ground, and the mind was wholly occupied in grasping at the luminous and beautiful forms which were made to pass over the imagination. In this state of feeling the suggestions of Satan became more rapid and distinct, until they were imbodied in a regular system. At this stage of the transaction, Satan appears in a visible form, adapted to the temper and feelings of his victim, doing no violence to his natural taste, but assuming an air of dignity and authority, blended with seeming kindness, and proffers his terms of treaty on a scroll, in the form of interrogatory, in substance as follows:

First. Have you a supreme contempt for the laws and authority of God?

Secondly. Are you disposed to resist his will, and gratify your own?

Thirdly. Do you reject the Scriptures so called, as containing unjust and unreasonable requirements?

Fourthly. Do you contemn and despise the sacraments and institutions of God?

Finally. Do you surrender yourself, soul and body, to my service, to be employed in whatever way I may judge conducive to the progress of my kingdom among men?

These questions, and others like them, are accompanied by a statement of immunities and privileges which Satan promises to confer in case the party gives his assent, and pledges himself to fidelity in all parts of the compact to the best of his ability. The advantages to be conferred on the part of Satan are as follows:

First. He promises to preserve his subject from all personal danger, for having entered into this contract.

Secondly. To allow him free indulgence in whatever sins may be most agreeable to his taste and disposition.

Thirdly. To invest him with new faculties, by which he may enter the spiritual world, and hold communion with kindred spirits, who inhabit the regions of the air.

Fourthly. To give him power over the bodies and minds of others, that he may torment and perplex them, and then free them from disquietude and pain, on condition that they will come over to his service.

Finally. To give him honors and rewards in his kingdom, proportioned to the value of his services and the degree of his fidelity.

The terms being agreed upon, the solemn assent of both parties is given, and the bond is written in mystical characters, sealed with a black seal, and the miserable man signs it with a pen dipped in his own blood. After this, all fear of God, all dread of wrath, all sensibility of conscience, and every disposition to good cease for ever, and no renewing grace, no sanctifying influence can evermore visit that heart, which is thus abandoned of its Maker, and separated to all evil and misery for ever.

Such, continued the preacher, is the nature, and these are the terms of this dreadful confederacy. For its proof, we have only to refer to the facts and confessions that are daily passing under our observation. That Satan has come down upon us in great wrath, is no longer to be denied; that God, for wise but inscrutable reasons, has permitted this calamity to come upon the land, no one can doubt. These reasons in due time will be unfolded, and meanwhile we may be assured that our sins as a community have done much to provoke God, our rightful governor, to leave us a prey to this 'roaring lion, who goeth about seeking whom he may devour.'[3]

But if any one denies that the confessions and statements which have been so often and solemnly made, are to be relied upon, we will refer them to an unerring record, an infallible proof that Satan possesses such power on earth. The plainest precepts of the Mosaic law recognized such wicked agencies, and provided for them summary and dreadful punishment. The first king of Israel worshipped at the altar of demons, and at the instance of a witch,[4] the holy Samuel stood before him. In the dim shadows of the invisible state, that venerable form, in distinct and solemn features, was presented to his eye, and in the strange and mystical tones of that unimagined state of being, denounced the death and ruin of himself and his house. As we come down to later times, we find in the days of our blessed Saviour, the presence and power of evil spirits,[5] and it was one of his offices of love to deliver men from this cruel bondage;

and in all succeeding times, we see traces of the same dreadful agencies, until at length, upon this land, consecrated to God, the visible footsteps of the destroyer are seen, and every means of expulsion which the Scriptures warrant, must be employed to drive him from our midst.

Having thus stated the nature and proof of this confederacy, he proceeded to point out the means by which the tempter might be resisted and overcome. These, he said, were obviously watchfulness, fasting and prayer. When a christian was faithful in these duties, there was little danger of being overcome by temptation, and he detailed at length, the times and seasons and the different points of character at which the assaults of Satan would be most successfully directed, and the various methods by which he might be repelled. He then showed that Satan could not, and never intended to perform his part of the contract; that so long as his subject was useful in his cause, he might defend and protect him; but the moment his affinity with the master spirit was detected and exposed, he seldom, or never interposed to save him from punishment. He then closed his discourse by the most passionate entreaties to his people, to guard against the wiles of the adversary; to watch and pray lest they entered into temptation; to repent of their sins, which had brought down the judgments of God on the land; and to be fruitful in those works of faith and labors of love which would prove the sincerity of their trust in God, and turn away from his heritage these tokens of his anger.

As Strale and his friends returned from church, the sermon was a fruitful theme of conversation. 'I could almost forgive Mr. Mather for his superstition,' said Walter, 'if it would hurt no one but himself.'

'And why pardon it in him,' said Mary, 'when you condemn it so much in others?'

'Because,' returned Walter, 'I admire his genius: it is grand and beautiful even in its illusions; he has the faculty of making rank folly appear like luminous and well-supported truth.'

'And it is the more criminal and dangerous for all this,' returned Mary; 'he reminds me of a beautiful stream, which in the distance is invested with a thousand charms. Its banks are arched with shades and bordered with flowers. Every thing is inviting and lovely; but when you approach, the rustling of the serpent among its bushes, and the poisonous green on its margin, show you that Death has planted his engines among that foliage, and hurls his arrows with destructive aim upon the unsuspecting traveller.'

'It is safe enough for me, Mary, to admire the beauty of that river, provided I see its dangers and avoid them; but I am fully aware of the justice of your views, and in the present state of public feeling, such a sermon may do inexpressible harm. I cannot doubt Mr. Mather's sincerity, but he ought to know better; he has the means of knowing better and is deeply responsible for the mischievous effects of such preaching. He has a wonderful faculty of making the worse appear the better reason, and clothing his own hallucinations in the garb of truth; but he will never be a safe man, and I dread his influence in our political circles.'

'We must deal with him in all charity,' said Mary; 'he aims to do good, and I have a prevailing opinion of his piety, though I must confess, the picture is shaded by many a sombre line.'

The young friends soon reached home, and agreeably to the pious custom of those days, each one retired to his chamber for meditation and prayer. These duties were kept up till nearly sunset, when the family assembled at the tea table, where no secular conversation was permitted to intrude. The evening was usually occupied in religious conversation or sacred music. On the present occasion, some appropriate selections were made from the version of Sternhold and Hopkins,[6] at that time used by the church of England, and the sweet voices of the young maidens gave utterance to strains of melody which for culture and expression, were seldom heard in the primitive days of New England.

The later hours of the evening were spent in the garden. The moon was riding with her starry train, in peerless beauty above them. The fragrance of the apple blossoms filled the air, and the sweet tranquillity of a Sabbath eve came down upon this lovely circle of friends, as they contemplated that better land, whose vivid emblems were shining above and around them.

CHAPTER ELEVENTH

THE BEAUTIFUL MONTH of June was now spreading its green ornaments over the face of New England. Never did the early summer unfold a more luxuriant foliage, or cover the fields with a fresher beauty, than that which now adorned the land. The forests and gardens were vocal with the music of birds, the rose and violet came forth in unwonted fragrance, and a cloud of incense went up from every valley and hill, to the praise of their Creator and Lord. The world of nature was moving on in perfect harmony and beauty. But the world of mind was in ruins, its stately palaces had fallen, Reason was dethroned, and a dark mass of chaotic elements moved over its surface in mingled confusion and horror. Spirits of evil were riding on the blast, unnatural and distorted shapes occupied every field of thought and reflection, and Superstition held in her mighty grasp whatever element opposed her power, and scowled in triumph and scorn over a perverted understanding and a misguided conscience.

On the 10th of June, 1692, the first victim of this mournful delusion died at the scaffold and by the hands of the public executioner.[1] Her indictment stated, that she had made a covenant

with Satan, and in obedience thereto, was engaged in the practice of wicked arts, to the great annoyance of godly persons. The
nature of these practices was described at length, and consisted
in the infusion of wicked and devilish thoughts into minds hitherto pure and uncorrupt, in the infliction of sharp pains on the
hands, the neck and the limbs of the sufferer, in various temptations to assist the devil in his nefarious designs upon the peace
and order of society, and in promises of future rewards if the
party would consent to become a subject and servant of Satan.

A company of nervous and agitated witnesses supported the
indictment, by testifying to the power she exerted over their minds
and bodies, and the wild actings of their own fanaticism, and its
physical effects, were imputed by them to a mysterious energy
derived by the supposed witch from the master of apostate spirits. On such evidence as this, she was condemned by the highest
court in New England, and, by a sentence most unjust and cruel,
was consigned to an ignominious death. As the multitude, who
witnessed the execution, retired from the dreadful spectacle, it
was only to tremble for themselves and for each other: even the
pleadings of mercy and the voice of pity were suppressed, and
those who dared to intimate a belief in opposition to the prevalent
opinions, were the first to be suspected and arrested.

On the evening of this day, two persons were seen on their
way to the house of Mr. Parris, the clergyman of Danvers,[2] at
that time called 'Salem village.' One of these was a young man
of genteel appearance, and the other a female, whose dress was
that of a country maiden, but whose sharp countenance and cunning, selfish aspect denoted that she was intelligent beyond her
apparent condition. The conversation was earnest and vehement
on both sides; and as they approached the house, the slowness of

their pace indicated that their plans, or purposes, were not fully matured.

'This business looks too serious to me,' said the female; 'I hardly dare undertake it. Miss Graham must be innocent; and how can I be the cause of her death?'

'Did you not say,' said Trellison, 'that she had been the cause of constant torment and vexation; that she controlled your movements, and by a look suspended your purposes; that in her presence, you would weep or smile, without any cause whatever? Moreover, did you not see her at that cursed sacrament of devils, where every vow is sealed by blood, and where she solemnly ratified the hellish compact? What are all these but proofs of her damnable affinity with Satan? You cannot go back. The Lord requires your service, and it must be done.'

'But, Mr. Trellison,' replied the female, 'if I take this course, what will become of me? I shall be shunned by the good; and if Miss Graham is acquitted, where shall I find recompense and security?'

'Have I not told you of recompense? Is it nothing to free the world from the possessed of Satan? Is it nothing to foil the great adversary of soul and body? Is it nothing to free yourself from these annoyances? Is it nothing, Clarissa, to save your own life?'

'My own life—what is that worth, Mr. Trellison, if the mind is loaded with conscious guilt? Even now, I start at every shadow, and imagine a foe in every one I meet. And what is the amount of this victory over Satan, as you call it? Why it seems to me, such a victory would be my ruin. But I have started in the race, and fate seems to press me onward. I may be doing God service. Will you, Mr. Trellison, pledge yourself that my reward shall be reasonable and sure?'

'I have pledged my word, and the assurances of all the faithful are yours, that whatever injury any one suffers in this righteous cause, shall be fully recompensed. You shall be rewarded.'

They now separated as they approached the house, and Clarissa, who had been fully instructed in the part she was to act, entered the kitchen, and took her place with the servant, with whom she had long been acquainted. Trellison, as he entered the parlor, saw Mr. Parris, through an open door, seated in his library alone. They had long been familiar acquaintances, and though the clergyman was many years his senior, yet he was fully aware of the reputation of his friend for piety, and had known him personally since his first entrance at Harvard College. After some desultory conversation, the mournful events of the day were called up, and Mr. Parris remarked, that he looked back upon its scenes with extreme agitation and horror. 'Surely, Mr. Trellison,' said he, 'it was a dreadful sacrifice. But how could it be avoided?'

'It was a sacrifice well pleasing to the Lord,' said Trellison. 'Why start, Mr. Parris, at the sternness of the divine command? Must our pity overcome our sense of obligation?'

'No indeed,' said Mr. Parris; 'and here is the bitterness of the trial. He that putteth his hand to the plough, is forbidden to look back:[3] but how can I behold such misery without a tear of pity?'

'When Abraham was commanded to slay his son,' said Trellison, 'he laid him on the altar and took the knife in his hand. Was there any misgiving? Doubtless pity moved his heart; but his hand was true to the divine mandate, and he only forbore at the express command of God.'[4]

'But are we equally sure, that God commands us to this work of violence? Might we not by prayer disarm the Tempter, and drive him from our midst?'

'Faith without works is dead;[5] and how can we expect the blessing of God, but in the use of means? Shall Satan rage in our land, and the servant of God remain idle at his post? Every thing depends on the energy and zeal with which this arch-apostate is hunted and driven from his hiding places; and those, who harbor him and practice his wicked devices, must perish without mercy.'

'True, most true, Mr. Trellison: forgive the momentary, the sinful pity, which would, if indulged, unnerve my hand, and draw me back from the service of God. I would not shrink from my duty; but I am startled and confounded at the numbers who have engaged in this cursed league with Satan. They must be punished. You are aware, that a society has recently been formed for the discovery and punishment of witches. This scroll was brought to me to-day by a member, and all the persons on this list will be watched, and probably most of them arrested. If you know of other cases, where the charges can be supported by competent evidence, it will be my duty to present them to the society.'

Trellison took the list, which contained the names of seven or eight persons. Most of these had long been suspected; but the last name on the scroll was that of one, whose blameless life and holy profession had hitherto given him a high rank in the community. It was the Rev. George Burroughs, a minister of the gospel,[6] of the same religious faith as that of Mather, Parris and their associates, and perfectly exemplary in his deportment and conversation.

'And has it come to this?' said Trellison. 'Oh, the power of these hellish arts, that have profaned even the house of God, and turned the servant of Christ to a minister of Satan! But I can hardly credit what you say. Is the proof convincing?'

'Perfectly so,' said Mr. Parris. 'He was Satan's minister at that dreadful sacrament, in which most of those now in prison bound themselves to his service by their own signature, under the bloody seal. Moreover, he has the promise of being a prince in Satan's kingdom; and he took one of those faithful maidens, who have put their lives in jeopardy for the service of God, and carried her to a high mountain,[7] where, after the fashion of his master, he showed her the glory of the world, and promised to give her all, if she would but sign her name. But she wisely told him, those things were not his to give, and refused to sign. Such is the evidence against Mr. Burroughs. There is no alternative; we have canvassed the whole matter, and he must die.'

'So perish all the enemies of the Lord!' said Trellison. 'And now, Mr. Parris, there is yet one name to be added to that gloomy catalogue. Until now, I have not been nerved with strength to go forward in this divine work, and while my heart rebels at every step and my whole frame is convulsed with agony, I pronounce the name of Mary Graham.'

Mr. Parris started from his seat.[8] 'Such a name, and from you, Mr. Trellison?'

'Tremble not, my friend, nor wonder at what seems so strange. I have had such revelations from the Lord, such experience of her dreadful compact with the Prince of darkness, and such proofs from others who know her well, that, upon the peril of my soul, I dare not disobey a voice louder than seven thunders to my ears. Miss Graham is bound over to Satan!'

'I cannot credit your assertions, Mr. Trellison: Miss Graham is above all suspicion. If such a mind is affected by this dreadful influence, who of us shall escape?'

'Nevertheless you must,' said Trellison. 'I was once held in bondage by her magic arts: but, thanks to God, my soul is now at liberty; escaped, as a bird out of the snare of the fowler. But

others are still entangled in her yoke of bondage, and they must
be liberated. Some of our students have fallen under her power,
and under this roof is one who is daily persecuted by her devices. Clarissa Snow, the faithful servant of Mr. Ellerson, is now
here, and will tell you in person what she has suffered.'

'Oh, righteous God!' said Mr. Parris, 'spare me this heavy
blow! let not thy wrath wax hot against thy servant;[9] and if this
work of judgment must proceed, consign it, I beseech thee, to
other hands, and let no more blood be found in my skirts!'[10]

'What means this language?' said Trellison. 'Has not God
vouchsafed to you his peculiar presence and blessing? has he
not revealed to you these mysteries of iniquity, and made you
the honored instrument of bringing to light the hidden things of
darkness? will you pause in the work to which he calls you?'

'I cannot pause,' replied Mr. Parris; 'but I know not how to
proceed. Once more, I appeal to Heaven for the rectitude of my
purposes; and if I am the chosen instrument to sweep the chaff
from his threshing floor, I can only say—Oh God, thy will be
done![11] let me not turn back from this work; let me not blench
in this terrible conflict with the powers of darkness; let me not
turn my hand from the shedding of blood, till a voice from the
excellent Glory tells me to forbear!'

'And now,' he added, 'your testimony shall be examined, and
if it be such as the revelations of God to my own soul shall approve, Miss Graham, whatever may be the consequences, must
be arrested.'

In a few moments, Clarissa was introduced, and to the several questions that were asked, she replied in such a manner as
confirmed the statements of Trellison. She complained of various torments in the presence of Miss Graham, which torments

ceased when she was absent. She also complained of dark purposes and evil thoughts, which always vanished when Miss Graham was out of sight.

It is not necessary to repeat more, for the credulous clergyman was easily convinced; and moreover, these results accorded with those inward revelations which to him were conclusive evidence of her guilt; and he now, though with a trembling hand, added her name to the list of victims.

This was but the first step in the dark machinations of Trellison. He knew the ground he occupied was treacherous: but confiding in the strength of the public delusion, and perhaps believing, in part, he was doing God service, he was emboldened to proceed and carry on his designs of blood. In the picture, which the conversation we have related gives of his character, the lines are deepened to an uncommon shade of guilt. But in the midst of the revenge he sought, there were feelings of gloomy fanaticism, which probably concealed from his own view the enormity of his purposes, and even clothed them with a false lustre. He was a believer in these compacts with Satan; and the very unaccountable testimony of credible witnesses had led him to look upon those who practiced witchcraft, as persons who must be cut off, and the land be purged, in this way, from the demons who had broken loose upon it. Yet in the midst of all, there must have been moments, when the accuser Conscience broke in upon his refuge of lies, and upbraided him with a purpose, which came nearer to the acts of Satan, than any which visible evidence had yet developed.

CHAPTER TWELFTH

Soon after the return of Lyford from Hadley, Strale having no longer any special occasion for Pompey's services, determined to give him his liberty, in advance of the time specified by his father. He accordingly informed Pompey that he now wished him to enjoy the luxury he had so long desired, that of being his own master. Walter furnished him with a small sum of money, and Mr. Gardner assured him he should have employment about the wharf at reasonable wages. Pompey was in raptures in the possession of his newly acquired liberty, and for many days his enjoyment was unbounded. But he had no notion of being employed as a laborer; and having procured a fashionable hat, with silk stockings and a coat well covered with gilded buttons, and silver buckles on his shoes, Pompey strutted up and down King street for a month or more, to the great amusement of the shop keepers, and with such vast opinions of his own consequence, as no amount of ridicule could possibly diminish. But the golden dream could not last always; it was not broken, however, till the last penny of his cash had disappeared, when he awoke to the consciousness that he had played the fool, and that his pretensions to the character of a gentleman of leisure must be abandoned. In this condition, he had recourse to Strale as his only friend, and begged him to find employment for him on a farm, at a distance from town, where he was willing to go back to his old habits of labor and care. Walter had taken no pains to arrest him in his course of folly, believing that experience was the only cure for his extravagant dreams; but he was very willing to assist him in any way, that might promote his good, and accordingly procured for him a situation on a farm in Danvers, occupied by Mr. Putnam, a highly respectable man,[1] who promised to watch the motions and check the follies of Pompey, as much as might be in his power.

It was a new and not very agreeable scene to Pompey. He had no chance for the display of authority; but was ordered to mind his own business, whenever he presumed to step out of his sphere. This life of discipline was too severe to be endured, and he gradually became remiss in his labors, until at length, it required the constant exercise of authority to induce him to labor at all. In this condition, he contrived various methods of escape from a post that was every way disagreeable; but he well knew, that if he left Mr. Putnam without good reason; he had nothing further to expect from Walter. Happily for him, as he thought, the witch delusion was now advancing with a power which nothing could resist; he saw the influence and importance which had been gained by the impostors who pretended to be afflicted; and there seemed no way so likely to mend his fortunes as to be afflicted himself, and then turn informer.

With a view to carry out this policy, Pompey went to Mr. Parris and entered a complaint against his master. He declared, that Mr. Putnam tormented him night and day, and that strange things were going on at the farm; that one morning a field of grass was cut without hands, and the hay was put into the barn, perfectly dry in one hour after cutting; and that only the day before, as he was at work loading hay, Mr. Putnam stood at a long distance from him, with a hayfork in his hand, and that, in a mysterious manner, the fork entered his arm, inflicting a severe wound, the effects of which were now visible. These wonderful events excited the astonishment of the clergyman, who sent for the farmer, and requested his attendance on the afternoon of the next day.

A few minutes after Trellison's departure, the farmer entered the room, and found his minister in a reclining posture, and apparently absorbed in deep meditation. 'I have come,' said he, 'Mr. Parris, in obedience to your summons, and wish to know your pleasure.'

'Satan is among my flock, Mr. Putnam, and as the good shepherd careth for his sheep, I have feared you may be entangled in his wiles.'

'In my belief, and I am sorry to say it,' said the farmer, 'Satan has more to do with the minister than among the people.'

'Dare you speak thus to the Lord's ambassador, his commissioned and anointed servant, whom he has clothed with the helmet of salvation, and the shield of faith, that he may quench the fiery darts of the devil?'[2]

'You claim a high character, Mr. Parris; but I have heard of wolves in sheeps' clothing, and the course you are pursuing, leaves me in little doubt whose servant you are.'

'What other language than this is to be expected from those who have signed the black book, and eaten the sacrament of devils? You have sold yourself to the service of Satan, and these are the cursed fruits of your compact; it was to question you on

this point, that I sent for you to-day, and you owe it to my for-
bearance, that your name is not now on the scroll of the accused.
I wished to know whether the evidence of your servant Pompey
could be relied on. Your own language now convinces me of its
truth, and you will soon reap the wages of your iniquity.'

'I well know,' replied Mr. Putnam, 'how little evidence it takes
to satisfy you, when you are resolved to carry out your purposes.
Your own inward convictions, you say, support the evidence of
my servant. It will, however, be well for you to inquire, how far
his testimony may be trusted. I have brought him with me, that
you may question him in my presence.'

'It is a grace you do not deserve, but to show you my forbear-
ance and lenity, I will admit and question him now. You shall not
be condemned without a hearing.'

This concession from Mr. Parris was sudden and unexpected;
but he knew the sturdy character of Putnam, his excellent reputation, and the danger of pushing matters to extremity. He was
therefore glad of the opportunity to come down from the high
ground he had taken, and to assume the appearance of fairness
and liberality.

Pompey was now introduced, and the poor African was in no
very enviable position, between the two inquisitors; but he made
the best of his circumstances, and sat down quietly to undergo
the examination.

'You seem to be in a calmer state to-day, Pompey,' said the
clergyman; 'I hope the cause of your trouble is removed.'

'Witch gone, Massa Parris, all gone; Pompey well as ever.'

'Thanks be to God!' said the clergyman; 'he has heard my
prayer. I wrestled with him a full hour on your account, and he
gave me faith to believe that the devil would be cast out.'

'Massa Putnam got the witch out; he did it all himself—nobody helped him.'

'What do you mean, Pompey? I do not understand you.'

'I must now explain,' said Putnam, 'and am willing to apologize for the language I used when I came in, so far as to express my belief that you are under a strong delusion, and I do not wish to impute to you corrupt and wicked motives. You have been a good minister, and a kind man in past years, and you well know that in the contest for your parish rights, I have taken your side and supported your claims; but in these witch prosecutions, I have been astonished at the madness of your course, and can only account for it on the ground that you are partially insane; and now in regard to the change in Pompey, I will tell you all the facts. I went out this morning to oversee some men whom I had employed to dig a well. Pompey was there, dancing about in strange attitudes, and presently he threw himself on the ground and began to bite the roots of a tree, and fill his mouth with gravel. I asked him the cause of his strange conduct, and his only reply was, 'Witch, Massa, witch got into Pompey.' '

' 'Who put the witch in, Pompey?' was my next question.'

' 'You, Massa; all well, when you go away.' '

' 'Well, Pompey,' said I, 'if I made you sick, I ought to cure you. The same person who put the witch in, ought to drive the witch out;' and taking him to a tree, I gave him, at least, forty stripes, every one of which seemed to possess a magic power. The witches fled in every direction, and I have brought him to you to-day, clothed, and in his right mind. Now, Mr. Parris, I would not detract from the efficacy of your prayers; you know my reverence for religion; but in my poor opinion, if you would take those four wicked girls, (one of whom, I grieve to say it, is my niece, and bears the honest name of Putnam), and apply the same remedy which has done so much for Pompey, no sign of witchcraft would be seen, and the community would be restored to reason and common sense.'

So saying, the farmer took his departure with Pompey, leaving the minister to his own reflection, and to the deep mortification and shame, in which his own credulity and folly had involved him.

The position of Mary Graham was now critical and alarming. Since her return to Salem, she had boldly condemned the witch proceedings, and in every circle where she moved, her whole influence was directed against the prevailing delusion. Unappalled by the dangers that surrounded her, she extended her sympathy and pity to those who were in prison, and favored the escape of some who were in imminent danger of arrest. In these offices of love and charity she was nearly alone; for though her friends admired her courage and fortitude in the cause of humanity, yet few of them dared to imitate her example. She wrote to Walter and her brother, begging them in concert with Mr. Willard to see Dr. Mather, who had returned from England,[3] and enlist his influence to suspend all further prosecutions. But this good man, though he deplored the excesses into which the community was rushing, either believed the evil would soon be cured, or was so far influenced by his son, that he could not be induced to take a bold stand against the courts; yet it is believed he used much private remonstrance and expostulation, and it was generally supposed the public movements had none of his countenance and support.

Walter replied to Mary's letter, and informed her that no measure had been left untried with Sir William Phips and his advisers, but nothing could be done; the delusion had seized the minds of the most gifted men in the land, and it was vain to hope for relief until the public malady had run its course; and he expressed his fears that her own standing in society, and the general esteem in which she was held, might not prove a sufficient protection against the envy and malice of some, and the credulity and superstition of others. He expressed his admiration of the course she had taken, but in the present violent stage of the delusion he thought it would be best for her to retire from active participation in any remedies which might be applied, as they could not benefit others and might be attended by the worst consequences to herself.

Stoughton's court was now in full operation. His associates were Gedney,[4] Winthrop, and Sewall. This court was confessedly illegal, but the urgency of the occasion was considered a sufficient warrant for its organization. It was, in fact, an exparte tribunal, as all the judges were known to favor the superstition, and the only hope for those who were brought before it was in the jury, who were so perplexed and overawed, as in general to conform their verdicts to the known opinions of the court.

While affairs remained in this state, there was little prospect of relief from courts and judges. No other hope remained than that the delusion would soon show itself in forms so extravagant and revolting as to excite the contempt and rouse the indignation of the public. This conviction soon reached the mind of Miss Graham, and she forbore to remark upon the subject with her accustomed freedom. In fact it was no longer safe to ridicule or condemn; and with all her popularity and the universal esteem in which she had been held, it was evident she was now regarded with distrust and suspicion. Mr. Ellerson, whose views in general agreed with those of Mary, was extremely guarded and cautious, and often suggested to her his fear that she spoke with too little reserve. In fact, she was soon painfully convinced on this point: many of those whom she loved, began to withdraw from her society, and in various methods discovered their coolness and reserve. She was no longer welcomed with the smile of confidence and affection, and her evening walks, in which she was usually attended by several young ladies and gentlemen, were either wholly omitted or kept up in solitude. This change of the public feeling towards Mary was equally sudden and startling. She was unable to perceive the causes, or trace the insidious agents, who were fastening their toils around her. Neither explanation nor satisfaction could be had, and the mysterious reserve still gathered and increased, wherever she went. Some of her friends, particularly the Higginsons, confessed they dared not be seen in her society, while they privately assured her that their friendship was unabated, and begged she would still regard them with confidence and love.

There was a beautiful walk on the ground now occupied by the Salem Common[5] and the buildings on its left, in the direction towards Beverly. This was a favorite resort for Mary, a place where she indulged in many a happy contemplation on the works of nature, and the wonders of Providence: here too, in the sweet interchange of sympathy and affection with her young companions, she found sources of innocent and unalloyed satisfaction, and sometimes when alone, as she penetrated the depths of the forest and sat down on the green border of the rivulet, or under the shade of the magnificent elm, she realized what the poet many years after sung, in numbers that will never cease to move the contemplative and pious mind:

> 'The calm retreat, the silent shade
>   With prayer and praise agree;
> And seem by thy sweet bounty made,
>   For those who follow thee.'[6]

Though forsaken in great measure by her friends, Mary continued her visits to this chosen retreat, and there, in pensive recollection of other days, and a humble trust in Providence, she found solace and support for her disturbed and anxious mind. Mr. and Mrs. Ellerson, conscious of her innocence, did every thing in their power to soothe her feelings and sustain her sinking courage, but her sensitive mind drooped under the cold neglects of the world, and she even imagined that Walter's letters, though written in all the warmth of affection, began to show symptoms of coldness. Mr. Ellerson thought it his duty to inform Lyford of the state of things, and request his immediate attendance at Salem: this was accordingly done without her knowledge, and on the evening of the twenty-sixth of June,[7] she found herself in the arms of her affectionate and sympathizing brother.

Lyford was soon convinced that some deep laid plan had involved Mary in the suspicion and distrust of the community; but while he trembled at the dangers which surrounded her, his first object was to soothe her feelings, by the kindest offices which affection could suggest, while he constantly revolved in his mind the most probable methods for her deliverance. He wrote immediately to Strale, concealing none of the difficulties and dangers of the case, but requesting he would not now visit Salem, as he feared it might increase the danger, and excite a greater watchfulness against any means that might be devised for her escape.

The next evening, Lyford and his sister walked together and visited the place which was so much endeared to her, by its many delightful associations. It was a fitting occasion to reveal all her griefs, and Lyford no longer wondered at the unbroken sadness of her feelings. She informed him, that as she walked on the borders of a little stream in the forest, she had several times heard voices, pronouncing her real name, and sometimes accompanied by a soft strain of music, inviting her to new habitations among the immortals, and making promises of every kind of enjoyment, if she would but consent to join a company of spirits now on a visit to earth, and offering her distinctions and honors in a new kingdom, which was about to be established in the world. In conclusion, she had no doubt a conspiracy had been formed against her reputation and life, and she believed Trellison had set in motion these unseen agencies, which she feared would soon betray her to prison and death.

'And now, dear brother,' said she, 'what can I do? friends have deserted me on every side; wherever I turn, I meet no response to the most common offices of friendship and good will. When the Sabbath comes, that day of holy rest, whose heavenly influences have fallen so peacefully on my heart, it brings no relief to my troubled spirit: in the very temple of God, I see nothing but averted faces or disturbed looks, and I go and come more lonely and neglected than even the sparrow, who finds a nest for herself among the altars of God.'[8]

'I know not what it means,' said James; 'I am sure, Mary, it is not safe for you to remain here, and yet to attempt flight would probably be followed by instant pursuit, and go to confirm the suspicions that already exist. I shall not leave you, but we will consult together, and our earnest prayers must go up to Heaven for light and deliverance.'

'I have thought, James,' said Mary, 'that it is no longer of any use to conceal my name. The purpose intended by this conceal-ment has been answered; and though it may prejudice my cause still more with the authorities at Boston, yet, in my present cir-cumstances, I wish there may be no ambiguity or deception in any part of my conduct: besides, it is already known to some extent, for it has been repeated in yonder woods in my hearing.'

'You are right, Mary,' replied her brother. 'I believe more good than evil will result from the disclosure: I will get Mr. Ellerson to mention the facts to a few of his friends, and they will soon become generally known; but dear Mary, do not sink under this load of sorrow;[9] Walter and myself will love you even unto death. It is a dark day, but light may arise, and I feel assured that your deliverance will in some way be effected.'

'Ah! my brother,' said Mary, 'I would that such a hope could send its reviving influence to my heart, but I have the most gloomy anticipations and painful forebodings of the result. As I was walking, a few evenings since, by the side of this beauti-ful stream, I was enabled to cast my eye forward to the land of perfect and eternal repose; the lovely images of nature reflected to my mind the glories of the heavenly world, and I longed to put on the garments of immortality and walk among those pleas-ant landscapes, where the storms of trouble never blow. But the strife will soon be over, and 'mortality will then be swallowed up of life.' '[10]

'Why speak so mournfully, dear Mary? This world is not yet a desert, which no flower of hope nor green beauty of summer can adorn. Winter may come with its frost, but spring will return and bring freshness, blossoms and life in its train. There is a bright side to the picture; do not refuse to behold it.'

'Hush,' said Mary, 'hear you not the voices in yonder forest?' James paused, but no sound reached his ear. The wind sighed mournfully along, as if in sympathy with the sadness which had fastened deeply on the minds of brother and sister, as, arm in arm, they walked on the borders of the forest.

'Listen again,' said Mary; 'surely you must hear them, James.'

A low strain of music, like a faint chorus of voices, now fell upon his ear; in a moment it swelled to a distinct sound and sent its notes of melody among the valleys and rocks. A few words only of the first and second verses were distinguished, but every sound became more clear and impressive, until the following lines were distinctly understood:

> 'ON the bright and balmy air,
>   On the summer clouds we ride,
> From our golden realms we bear
>   Jewels for our master's bride.
>
> 'Mary, in the bowers above,
>   Sweetest groves of fairy land,
> We will crown thee Queen of Love,
>   Princess of the fairy band.
>
> 'Where the living palm-trees grow,
>   Where the crystal waters glide;
> Realms untouched by want or wo,
>   Thou shalt be our master's bride.
>
> 'Far below the sunny waves,
>   We have gems and jewels rare,

Pearly grots and coral caves,
    Thou shalt be our mistress there.'

At this stage of the music the words became inaudible, until the sound died away in the forest, and the quiet stillness of the evening again rested on the landscape.

'These are strange things, Mary,' said her brother, 'but they are only a part of the snares which are intended to betray you. Time will soon disclose all; meanwhile, have courage, my dear sister; in your conscious rectitude you will find consolation and support; in God there is abundant strength, and what man can do shall be faithfully done. Have no distrust of Walter; his love to you is all you can desire; he would be here to-day but for my cautions and warnings. As the danger thickens around you, we will watch and protect you at every step; but let us not trust in ourselves; it is not to be denied that your danger is great, and I am now of opinion that immediate flight is necessary: we will consult our friends to-night, and what we do must be done quickly.'

They soon returned home; it was too late for any hope of flight, and that very evening, Mary Lyford, by a warrant from the magistrate, was placed in the custody of the sheriff, to await her trial for the practice of witchcraft and sorceries.

CHAPTER THIRTEENTH

THE NEWS OF Miss Lyford's arrest, and the disclosure of her real name, produced a deep sensation in the community. The victims of this delusion had been hitherto taken from the lower walks of life, and this first attack upon the high places of society, while it shocked the feelings of many, served to reconcile the populace to the action of the courts, as it indicated that no influence of wealth or standing would be allowed to protect the guilty from punishment. Such was the state of the public mind, that except among Mary's immediate friends, no effort was made, or contemplated, for her deliverance. The sin of witchcraft was of too deep a dye to be forgiven; and the common doctrine was, that religion itself must turn away from such deadly foes to God and man. When the warrant was served, she was immediately removed from her friends, and placed in the care of an officer, who was directed to furnish an upper room in his house for her reception, and to guard her with ceaseless vigilance. There was little occasion for this warning, for the officer, whose name was Harris, would have thought himself bound over to perdition, had he suffered any prisoner in charge for a crime so enormous, to

escape. All access to Miss Lyford was forbidden, except to her
brother and Mr. and Mrs. Ellerson, who, assured of her innocence, did not scruple to express to the officer the utmost indignation and horror, at the violence thus done to one of their own
family.

It was scarcely possible to realize the change which the period of a single month had produced. The whole affair of Mary's
arrest and confinement seemed so like a dream, that they could
hardly persuade themselves of its reality. But in a short time
they saw the full extent of her danger, and had little doubt her
death would be demanded by the populace, and that the court,
whatever might be its wishes, would not dare to refuse the victim. The kind of evidence which was then current and considered valid, was so completely interwoven with every feature of
her case, that her guilt, in the public view, was already proved.
In these circumstances, Mr. Ellerson and his lady forbore to
excite the populace, by public denunciation; but in their own
circle of high respectability and influence, they were loud in
their demands for her release, and insisted that some sinister
motive had betrayed her into the toils of the accuser.

Lyford had accompanied his sister to the jailer's room, where
he provided every convenience which the rough and superstitious keeper would allow. For several days before her arrest,
Mary had been prepared for the worst; and she calmly resigned
herself into the hands of the law, to await an issue, which she
from the first apprehended would be fatal. There was no visible
emotion in her countenance, but a deep melancholy had fallen
upon those lovely features, which in their mild and beautiful, yet
pensive and solemn aspect, would have excited in any heart, not
steeled by fanaticism, the liveliest interest and sympathy. No ray

of light could penetrate the cloud that shaded her earthly hopes, and her spirit was now struggling to free itself from worldly ties, and to move in a calmer region, beyond this stormy and distracted world.

The next day after Mary's arrest, Lyford returned to Boston, to communicate the tidings to Walter, and prevent any rash or violent measure, to which his vehement temper might prompt him. No language can describe his feelings, when the facts were disclosed by Lyford; but the strong excitement of his mind was soon subdued by the calm remonstrances of his friend, who assured him that every thing depended on coolness and deliberation. Walter immediately laid upon himself the most severe restraints, and while he vowed to effect her deliverance, or perish in the attempt, he soon became so entirely the master of his own feelings, that no perceptible change was visible in his deportment. His first impulse was to proceed directly to Salem; but Lyford convinced him that such a step would be worse than useless, as he would not be permitted to see Mary, and it might throw serious obstacles in the way of her escape. It was therefore concluded he should remain at home, and that no interview with Mary should be attempted, but through the medium of her brother.

The trial of Miss Lyford took place about the middle of July.[1] Several witnesses were examined, whose testimony was considered conclusive of her guilt. Clarissa, Mr. Ellerson's servant, testified to the strange influence she exerted over her, and even in court took care to exhibit one of those remarkable fits of agitation and nervous excitement, which were universally satisfactory to the judges. Another witness declared she had seen Miss Lyford walking alone in the neighborhood of the forest, and that mysterious voices were heard in the woods, and unearthly music, and she remembered and repeated some lines, which intimated that she had consented to become one of a band of spirits, on account of which, she was soon to be crowned queen of a new kingdom, and to receive an untold amount of riches. Other testimony of a similar character was produced, but Trellison took care not to appear in the case; he did not choose to involve himself in unnecessary difficulties, and was probably aware that revenge for his known disappointment might be assigned as a motive for his testimony, and thus defeat the great object he had in view.

Such was the nature and amount of the evidence, it was scarcely possible to expect an acquittal. The examination was indeed prolonged, beyond the usual time, perhaps with a view to give some notion of the lenity of the court; but when the case was given to the jury, they scarcely hesitated, and when the verdict was demanded, it was with a bolder voice than usual, that the foreman pronounced the fatal word, "Guilty!" There was a deep solemnity and silence in the thronged court room, though little sympathy was manifested for the unoffending and beautiful maiden, whose fate was now so certain. The public frenzy had sealed the fountains of compassion, and the judge soon after pronounced sentence of death, to be executed on the twentieth of the following August.

We have not yet spoken of the demeanor of Miss Lyford, during this fearful period. Suffice it to say, it was calm and dignified, worthy her illustrious descent, and adorned by every christian virtue. Her confidence was not in man; and though her ties to life were of the strongest character, she could contemplate death without dismay. The shock attending the trial and sentence was indeed great, but the gospel was present to her aid with its well-springs of consolation, its life of immortality, and 'its exceeding weight' of future and eternal glory.[2] Her eye of faith looked beyond the tempests of that awful night, whose fearful horrors thickened over her, and beheld the rising day of celestial glory.

The friends of Mary now sought from Gov. Phips, through the kind offices of his lady,[3] the executive clemency: but the faint hope they entertained of a pardon, soon died away in total despair. Sir William absolutely refused to interpose, and his purpose was strengthened by his knowledge of her name and descent, which were more odious to him, if possible, than her imputed witchcraft.[4] But when it came to be announced that the young lady hitherto known as Miss Graham, was a relative of the venerated Goffe, a feeling of sympathy and pity was strongly and generally manifested; but its public exhibition was soon hushed by a sense of personal danger; every one was too deeply concerned for himself, to bestow much solicitude upon the fate of others.

Other methods were now adopted, and high rewards were offered in private, to bold and adventurous men, if they would procure her escape from prison: but no one could be found of sufficient courage to make the effort. Walter then attempted to bribe the jailer; but that resolute officer would not be tampered with. He was too much concerned for his own soul, he said, to suffer a witch to escape. He redoubled his vigilance; other sentinels were also placed on guard, and no access to Miss Lyford was permitted, except an occasional visit from James, who now spent all his time at Salem; and even this boon was with great difficulty obtained.

On these occasions, James bore to his sister the most affecting memorials of Walter's continued love, and assured her of his belief that some way of escape would yet open, and that all his time and thoughts were employed in devising plans for her deliverance. Mary, however, placed little reliance on such deceitful grounds of hope, and remitted nothing of her endeavors to prepare for the awful scene that awaited her. It was indeed grateful to see such proofs of Walter's affection, in the midst of all the obloquy which had clouded her name, and made her the reproach and scorn of the community; but her ties to earth were loosening, the glorious visions of the heavenly rest absorbed her mind, and she looked beyond the troubled stream she must soon cross, to a land of undecaying beauty and eternal repose.

All the efforts of James and Walter were warmly seconded by the Ellersons; and in their frequent conversations, every suggestion that prudence could make, was carefully balanced and weighed. But it was reserved for the fertile invention of Strale, to devise the only expedient which seemed to offer the least chance of success; and though this was confessedly romantic and extremely difficult to manage, it was resolved to make the trial.

Near the house of Mr. Harris, who had charge of Miss Lyford, there was a small cottage, occupied by a poor but honest laborer, named William Somers. This man was an ardent admirer of Gen. Goffe, and had once seen and conversed with him at his retreat in Hadley. Moreover, he was a sturdy Puritan, and in high reputation for honesty and piety: no one ever questioned his integrity, and he was the last person to be suspected of any plot against the peace of the community. Somers was just the man for the present emergency; and as soon as Miss Lyford's name was publicly disclosed, he went to Mr. Ellerson, and volunteered his services in any proper measures for her release, assuring him he

might rely on his fidelity. There was little need of this assurance,
for Somers was never known to break his word or slight his engagements. The location of Somers' cottage was very favorable,
and in fact essential to the success of the plan, as no other house
near that of Harris could possibly be obtained. His offer of assistance was therefore gratefully accepted, and he was at once
admitted to the councils of Mary's friends. The progress of our
narrative will develope the means that were employed, and the
consequences that followed.

The policy now to be adopted, required that Walter should no
longer keep up his relations to Miss Lyford, and that he should
so far acquiesce in the public feeling, as to offer no vindication, or even suggest a wish in her behalf. It was no easy task to
pursue this line of conduct; but as it did not require a positive
disavowal of his engagement, he felt justified in assuming such
a degree of indifference to her fate, as might be necessary for the
successful prosecution of his designs.

Among Mary's friends in Boston, there were very few who did
not follow the fashion of the world, in deserting the unfortunate,
and leaving them to struggle alone in their wretchedness, without sympathy or consolation. Miss Hallam, Mary's earliest and
most intimate friend, was one of the first to forsake her. In fact,
this young lady was never pleased with the attentions which
were so liberally bestowed on Miss Lyford, and it was more than
suspected that her own attachment to Strale, reconciled her to
the impending fate of her friend. She saw, with scarcely dis-
guised pleasure, that Walter seemed to regard Mary with little
interest, and as he was now a frequent visiter at her father's, she
began to hope his affections were already enlisted in her behalf.
There were some, however, whose feelings and conduct were

far different. Among these, Miss Elliott was deeply affected at the situation of her friend, and did not hesitate to condemn the proceedings, as in the highest degree cruel and unjust. She made repeated visits to Mr. Willard, in the hope that he might do something in her behalf; and the benevolent clergyman employed all the power he possessed in her favor. She made the same application to Cotton Mather, but the stern fanaticism of this man was proof against all her entreaties. He declared he had no malice, and nothing but kindness towards Miss Lyford in his heart; but he solemnly believed in the allegations against her, and that God and man required the sacrifice. The proof he said was clear, and an exception in her favor would be cruelty to the community and treachery to his divine Master. All he could do was to pray, that notwithstanding her sorceries, she might, if possible, be forgiven, and he would not refuse her the tribute of a tear. Such were the feelings of this remarkable man, and such the power of superstition over his vigorous but ill governed mind. He was not naturally cruel, but in whatever devious course his perverted sense of duty impelled him, no consideration of reason or humanity could bring him back.[5]

Mean-while the days glided on, and the period was at hand when the fatal sentence of the law was to be executed. The nineteenth of August had been assigned for the death of Burroughs and three of his associates, who had been condemned on the same grounds. One female also had been selected, to complete the sacrifice.[6] For these unhappy individuals there was no hope of escape; the public voice had condemned them, as well as the iniquitous court before which they were tried; and they prepared, with christian resignation, for the doom which could not be averted. Miss Lyford's sentence had been assigned one day

later, as the case was deemed one of solemn and peculiar interest; and moreover it was the policy of the court to impress the
public mind with the enormity of the crime of witchcraft, by
repeating the tragedy in its most awful and startling forms. The
only hope that remained for Mary, was in those secret movements of her friends, which, in their complicated and delicate
machinery, might be frustrated by the severance of a single cord.
Her brother had acquainted her with the outlines of the plan, but
she had little faith in a prospect which seemed so visionary and
hopeless. Neither had Lyford any great confidence in its success, and every day had meditated some new expedient to ac-
complish her deliverance—but it was all in vain. No other hope
appeared; and when the eighteenth of August had arrived, Mary
was still in the custody of Harris, and that vigilant officer and
his three assistants, were the sleepless sentinels at their post of
dishonor and shame.

CHAPTER FOURTEENTH

'ACCURSED BE THE hour that gave me birth![1] Why was I born for this? Oh, thou insulted, yet forbearing God! if thine avenging justice pursues me to the lowest perdition, it will not outrun my crimes. Why did I hunt the innocent without cause, and heap on my soul such mountains of guilt? Oh, hide me, earth! bury me in thy deepest graves, if they will but shelter me from a raging conscience and a frowning God! How shall I save the innocent blood? how shall my feet, which have run so swiftly in the way of evil, turn back into the path of peace? These hands have built that fatal scaffold, on which innocence and virtue must perish! Oh, might I die in her stead! Oh, that my blood might expiate my guilt! Vain hope! the weight of mountains, the fires of the second death can neither crush nor consume me. Mine is an undying death, mine an unquenchable flame!'

Such were the exclamations of the wretched Trellison, as he stood on that fatal hill[2] with the scaffold which, the day before, had been erected under a tree, directly in his view. He was now fully awake to a consciousness of his crimes: he had betrayed into the hands of the law, one of the most innocent and virtuous of her sex, and was about to witness the awful consummation of his guilt. He had opened the door, but it was beyond his power to shut it. If he avowed the truth, his single testimony could not avail against the host of witnesses which his own arts had procured, and whose evidence, if now confronted by his, would in self-defence be combined to involve himself as well as Miss Lyford in ruin and death. In this condition, he thought of every possible method to avert the impending fate of Miss Lyford; but every avenue seemed to be closed; and after wandering up and down the hill for several hours, in the utmost horror and distraction of mind, he finally determined to follow her to the scaffold, and there avow his guilt, and invoke every power within his reach, to save her from the threatened doom.

It is often a mournful duty to display the workings of an accusing conscience. The picture may warn us to shun the incipient stages of guilt, and turn back into the current of reason and reflection the wild and turbulent elements of excited passion. Too often, alas! we plunge into the very vortex of ruin, ere we are conscious that we have passed the boundaries of virtue. Such is the influence of pride, self-love, and self-esteem, that the first discovery of guilt and danger, often comes too late to save us from the final plunge. This was preëminently the case with Trellison: with hasty and violent feelings, unguarded by reason, and driven by every wave of passion, he had mistaken his own purposes of revenge for zeal in the cause of religion, and had so blended his own selfish designs with an imagined regard for the honor of his Maker, as to conceal from himself his actual guilt, until its fatal effects stared him in the face, and revealed the depths of iniquity in which he was ingulfed.

When the next morning dawned, crowds of people were seen gathering round the spot, where the dreadful sacrifice which public fanaticism demanded, was to be made. Rev. George Burroughs and three other individuals, named Willard, Proctor, and Jacobs, together with one female, were taken from prison and conducted by the sheriff to the place of execution. The scene was one of appalling interest; and as the unhappy victims passed through the streets, loud murmurs of disapprobation were heard from many individuals, who believed they were mainly indebted for these tragical events to Boston interference, and who were indignant that Salem should be the chosen theatre for the display of these bloody scenes. The venerable Higginson, with several of his most influential parishioners, utterly refused all part in these proceedings, while his associate in the ministry, Mr. Noyes,[3] fully coöperated with Parris, Mather, and Stoughton, in all the length and breadth of this fatal delusion. When the hour of execution drew near, the public murmur became more loud and distinct, so much so as to excite alarm lest the purposes of justice might be frustrated. But at this moment Cotton Mather appeared on the ground, on horseback, and by the circulation of new proofs of Satan's promises and covenants with these unhappy persons, effectually silenced the voice of sympathy and the din of opposition. As the dreadful scene proceeded, Burroughs was seen kneeling on the scaffold in prayer, in which he solemnly appealed to his Maker for his uprightness of heart and his entire innocence of the crime for which he was called to die. He prayed fervently for himself and his hapless associates, thus performing in his last hours the kind offices of his sacred profession, and administering consolation to his fellow sufferers. Neither did he forget those bitter enemies who had brought him to this scene of horror; but earnestly supplicated their forgiveness from God, as he himself heartily forgave them.

Thus perished the persecuted Burroughs and his unhappy companions. They died as outcasts from God and man, their very names regarded with scorn and horror, and their persons execrated as the vilest of the vile. Time has lifted the veil; the storm of reproach has passed away; the shadows of the invisible world, in which they were seen to move as dark and mysterious forms enlisted in the service of Satan, and doing his will, have given place to the sunshine of Reason and Truth. The white robes of innocence and virtue now adorn them in the eye of every beholder, and that foul stain stamps with its darkest hues, the memories of Stoughton, Sewall, Gedney, and Cotton Mather.

Let it not be supposed there were no redeeming traits in the characters of these men. It was a superstitious age, and the delusions which were now abroad, had fastened with immense power upon the community at large; but this, though it may be urged in mitigation of their offences, was no valid excuse. They had unerring and sufficient maps in the experience of the past. They had the sure word of God. They had reason and common sense, which, impartial and unperverted, might have shown them the madness and cruelty of their course. These guides were consulted too late; and we have it recorded of Judge Sewall, that he deeply repented of his agency in these painful scenes, and publicly deplored his errors in the presence of the members of the South Church,[4] presenting his own example as a warning to future magistrates to avoid that fatal rock, on which justice and mercy had alike suffered shipwreck.[5]

It is probable Stoughton and Mather carried this delusion in part to their graves; and it is scarcely possible to contemplate these characters with complacency. There is no monument along the track of succeeding years, which redeems their memory from

its deserved reproach. Mather was learned and industrious beyond any man of that age in New England; but he was credulous
to the last degree; of a bold and fiery temper, deeply tinctured with
fanaticism, rash in his judgment, severe in his rebukes, and over-
bearing in his conduct. A cloud rests upon his memory, through
which Charity herself can scarcely discern the faint rays of real
piety, which, notwithstanding all his errors, probably existed in
his heart. Stoughton was, if possible, still more deeply implicated
in these cruel proceedings, and the remark of an eminent historian of Harvard College is undoubtedly just, that 'upon no individual did the responsibility of the sad consummation of that
excitement rest more heavily, than upon William Stoughton.'[6]

The next day was to be signalized by the death of Miss Lyford.
The public feeling was now so far subdued, that there was little
danger to be apprehended from the populace. If the death of
Burroughs had excited so little commotion, it was concluded
there would be no interruption to any future proceedings of the
like character. Moreover, there was a general belief that few cases of witchcraft had been more clearly defined, and the singular
language which had been addressed to her from the woods, and
was heard by others, was considered entirely conclusive in her
case. There had been no attempt to trace the cause of this strange
proceeding, but it was at once attributed to mysterious and spiritual agents; yet Lyford suspected what afterwards proved true,
that a female from Hadley, who knew his sister's history and
was in the confidence of her grandfather, had been employed by
Trellison in this work of deception; but he had no means of prov-
ing such a plot, and any attempt to implicate Trellison, who was
now in high favor with the ruling powers, would probably recoil
on himself, and lessen the chances of his sister's escape.

No access to Miss Lyford had been for some time permitted, except to her brother, and even this indulgence was now prohibited. Trellison found means, however, to convey to her a full confession of his guilt, his determination to avow it publicly, and if possible to stay the proceedings. He earnestly begged her forgiveness, and assured her that he wished to live no longer than to make a public vindication of her character, and save her if possible from her impending doom. This communication was not received till late in the evening, and it being impossible to obtain the favor of a light, or to procure the least office of kindness from her keepers, Mary was, of course, wholly ignorant of its contents. Her mind, also, was so fully occupied with the plans now in progress for her deliverance, that she was the less anxious to know its purport, and placing the paper in her bosom, the incident was nearly forgotten.

Trellison was involved in difficulties which so distracted his mind, that he was unable to devise any probable means, by which Miss Lyford's fate could be averted. His confessions and retractions, if made, he knew would only be regarded as new proof of her Satanic arts, and he now thought it safer to make his appeal to the populace and enlist their sympathies, than to attempt to stay a warrant which had been already issued, and could only be revoked by the Governor. Still he was unsettled in his plans, except that in the failure of all other means, he resolved to vindicate her at the scaffold, though it might cost him his life. The truth was, his convictions and remorse had arrived too late; and in the existing state of public feeling there was no proper light, in which evidence could be fairly seen; or if seen, its legitimate power could not at that time be felt. Strange as it may seem, the reports circulated by Cotton Mather on the preceding day had maddened the populace, and made them insatiate of blood. It was now believed that the death of Miss Lyford was essential to the public peace, and there was probably no moment in the progress of this delusion, when it ran higher, or was more terrible in its control over every generous feeling, than at this period.

Meanwhile, it was on the extravagance of this delusion that Miss Lyford's friends relied for her deliverance. The very feeling which Trellison feared would render his confessions unavailing, they were willing to provoke as the best means of her salvation. Mr. and Mrs. Ellerson no longer made any appeal in her behalf. Strale was in Boston, apparently unconcerned and unaffected, while Lyford alone kept his post near his sister, the only visible friend, from whom she could expect countenance or support.

There is that in human calamity, which, unsoothed by the voice of sympathy, and unrelieved by the kind offices of friendship, falls with a withering and consuming power on the heart. When such calamity is frequent and long continued, even the ties of kindred and affection are often sundered, and the unhappy sufferer, though conscious of rectitude, finds himself sinking in despondency, solitary and desolate, and his only support is drawn from the hope of a better world. Such emphatically was the condition of those who were proscribed for their supposed sorceries. Cut off from the sympathies of their fellow men, exposed to insult, violence, and death, and at last consigned to the scaffold, they were spectacles of unrelieved sorrow and wretchedness, of which the world can furnish few examples. But these unhappy victims did not forget their obligations to their fellow men and to God. They almost uniformly died in the spirit of forgiveness; and if, as the scoffer and the infidel allege, there be no hereafter, no review of character and responsibility, no discrimination between good and bad beyond this fleeting world, no probationary life here, and no retributory condition hereafter, then indeed is our faith vain, our works of love and charity are vain, and an unbroken gloom rests on the territories of the grave!

But the infidel forgets that the same chance which placed him in this world may not yet have exhausted its power. If it can move the world in its orbit, regulate the seasons, and govern, by irrepealable law, the motions of unnumbered suns and worlds, it may, for aught he can tell, act upon his future being; it may redeem the vital principle from the ashes of the tomb, and cast it among some new elements of life, which may be perfectly adapted to the work of retribution. Let him then beware of a theory which provides no security for his future happiness, while it reserves the right to perpetuate his being for ever; let him turn his eye to that even balance, in which his actions will be weighed,[7] and bring home to his heart the consolations which nothing but the gospel, approved, accepted, and trusted, can supply.

CHAPTER FIFTEENTH

ON THE EVENING of the nineteenth of August, a little schooner, which had occasionally stopped at the port of Salem, on trading voyages up and down the coast, entered the harbor. She was called the 'Water Witch,'[1] a fore-and-aft vessel of beautiful model and fine proportions. Whenever she was seen coming up the bay, crowds of people assembled to witness her movements. She was always kept in the best condition, and her nicely-trimmed sails, the perfect symmetry[2] of her spars, her graceful attitudes on the water, and above all, her rapid and varied motions, procured for Captain Ringbolt, who commanded her, an enviable and well-deserved reputation.

When the Water Witch appeared, it was always expected the next day would be one of extensive traffic, particularly among the country maidens of the neighborhood. Captain Ringbolt always had a good supply of laces, brocades, muslins, and all sorts of fashionable ornaments; and his very showy assortment was generally disposed of to good advantage. How he obtained his merchandise was sometimes a mystery;[3] but the Salem ladies were careful not to inquire too curiously into the matter; they were quite willing Captain Ringbolt should have his own way; and, as he was uniformly courteous and obliging, any suspicions would certainly be inexpedient, and perhaps unjust. It was rather wonderful, however, that so much charity was extended towards this gentleman, considering the very strict morals of the Puritans, and the rigid honesty with which they were accustomed to discharge their pecuniary obligations. The gallant captain generally told a good story, and, as our narrative all along supposes, there was no want of credulity among the people.

As the Water Witch dropped her anchor, Somers stood on the beach, watching her motions with deep interest and evident anxiety; one of his neighbors, named Bolton, who was also one of Miss Lyford's guards, having obtained leave of absence for an hour, was strolling near him, and remarked the closeness of his survey. Somers, absorbed in his own reflections, did not notice Bolton, till he touched him on the shoulder and said: 'What now, Somers? you are looking sharp for Ringbolt; what kind of traffic do you mean to drive with him?'

'Is this you, Bolton?' said Somers, in some confusion; but in a moment recovering himself, he added: 'These are perilous times, neighbor; the witch proceedings have stopped all business, and I thought, as there are not many fire-arms in town, if I could get all the pistols Ringbolt has, it might be a little speculation.'

'This Captain Ringbolt will soon grow rich,' said Bolton, 'if my guesses are right; he was here only two weeks ago, and sold all his cargo in two days. But he may come to a bad market now, unless he waits for better times before he sells his goods; he is a shrewd man, however, and sells things for a good price, when nobody else can sell at all. I wish I knew where he gets his articles. Neighbor Somers, I shall have nothing to do after the witches are hung; you know this captain—I wish you would try to get me a birth on board for the next voyage.'

'You are no more fit for a sailor, Bolton, than a monkey is to furl a topsail. Captain Ringbolt would tumble you overboard before you got ten leagues from land. You had better stay where you are, and find honester business than any I ever knew you to be employed about.'

'You are sharp this evening, Somers. You will one day be convinced that the man who watches criminals is doing a great favor to the community. But I cannot think what has brought Ringbolt back so soon; his vessel is light; I think he must have intended to be here this morning, and see how the devil hangs up his friends.'

'They had better send to the devil for a sheriff. And you, Bolton, are nearly right: a man must be more than half a devil, to be engaged in such business.'

'It is a truly godly business,' said Bolton, 'and I wonder at your language, Somers; if these witches will serve their master, they must take such wages as he gives them; and the wages of sin is death.[4] The sheriff deserves the thanks of all pious persons for his courage and zeal in the cause.'

'I wonder they had not employed you in the business,' said Somers; 'you talk like one who has no great compassion for a reputed witch, guilty or not guilty.'

'I am too sinful to be thus employed,' returned Bolton. 'I am not worthy, Somers, even to walk in the footsteps of those holy men, who are now purging the land of its sin and shame.'

'You are worthy,' replied Somers, 'to have a rope fastened to your neck, and to be swung from a gallows as high as Haman's.[5] What a wretch you are, Bolton, to see the innocent murdered around you, and exult in their death!'

'You must take care of your language, Somers, if you would save your own neck; there is to be another hanging to-morrow, and when that is over we shall want other victims; and your chance is getting to be a fair one. Why, if Mr. Parris, or Mr. Noyes, had heard half what you have said to me, you would be in prison this very night!'

'As to my own chance, it will be hard business to hang me up; but no thanks to you, Bolton, if it is not done to-morrow. You are under a strange delusion, and I must allow something for that. You were a good neighbor once, and I hope will be so again; but the time looks very distant to me. I am down this afternoon to get the first chance at Captain Ringbolt's assortment. Pistols, according to my way of thinking, will be in good demand; and I want something to defend myself with, and to put a shot or two into you, in case you should be an informer. At any rate, I am determined to have a first-rate pair for myself. You know I have some skill in the use of them. Will you go on board?'

'Not I,' said Bolton; 'I never go where pistols and powder are about, except when I use them in the holy cause. I hope you will think no more of what I said, Somers; you know I would not betray a friend.'

'There is no telling what you may do in such times as these; but there is little danger, so long as you are within reach of my pistol; beyond that, I would not trust you an hour. By the way, Bolton, have you no fears that Satan may carry you off, while you are hanging up his subjects? I wonder he does not appear in their behalf. If I believed as much as you do, I would not dare to stand guard over Miss Lyford.'

'I have weapons to fight him that you know nothing of, Somers. I have had some glimpses of him at twilight, but he saw me clothed in such armor that he dared not approach. I once met this same Apollyon[6] in the day-time, but only a small part of his dragon form was visible; and when I held up the holy gospels, he vanished into thin air.'

'If you should be called to grapple with him in person,' returned Somers, 'you would be more likely to make a treaty with him than to show fight. I am not sure, but it would be well for you to see what terms you can make with him; for I am well assured he will have his own terms by and by, and carry you off;—not that you are worth even the devil's acceptance, but because he is sent to look after such as you.'

At that moment Captain Ringbolt landed, and Bolton walked off, not exactly at his ease; for he knew that the honest and sturdy Somers was a dangerous enemy to such characters as he knew himself to possess; besides, it was time to resume his station as guard to Miss Lyford. 'I shall be released to-morrow,' thought he, 'and then I will make peace with Somers, and see if I cannot muster a little pity for the witch, and this will be sure to win his favor.'

Meanwhile, Somers went on board the Water Witch with Captain Ringbolt, and, entering the cabin, they conferred a short time, and soon settled the plan of operations. The crew of the schooner were entirely ignorant of Ringbolt's intended movements; and though a little suspicious that the voyage to Salem was not exactly of a trading character, they were so well trained and disciplined as perfectly to understand that nothing was to be said, even among themselves; all they had to do was to obey the orders of their superior.

Captain Ringbolt sent up his usual notices, which were posted in the streets, with an additional clause, stating that on account of the great event, which he trusted all godly persons would wish to behold on the morrow, he should not expose his goods for sale, till the day after, when, at the usual time and place, a most valuable assortment of articles, selected with great care, would be offered for sale. He returned thanks for the patronage he had received in past times, and assured the good people of Salem that no efforts would be wanting to merit their confidence, and meet the wishes of the public.

Somers walked away in sad contemplation on that state of things which seemed to make one delusion necessary to counteract and dispel another, which was far worse and more dangerous. But he was not quite satisfied with himself, especially with the kind of deception he had practiced on Bolton. The die, however, was cast. He implored pardon for the part he now felt compelled to act, and while he believed the extremity of the case, in the main, justified his course, yet it was so uncongenial to his feelings, and so opposite to the whole tenor of his life, that he was not a little disquieted by the scruples that oppressed him. He had a wife and one child. They were his earthly solace and hope, and his precautions, and those of Strale, had provided for their safety. For himself, the result was uncertain, but every possible contingency was guarded against, so far as human sagacity could foresee, or human skill provide.

The twilight had now fallen on the village and its surrounding scenes. The shadows deepened into uncommon gloom, as if Nature were spreading a funeral pall for the dead, and mourning over her deluded children and her own disregarded voice. Well might she sympathize in the sad desolation around her! Her own mighty impulses of gratitude and affection were silenced and suppressed by the mighty fabric of fanaticism and delusion, which occupied the throne of the intellect and the heart. Who shall assure us, that such scenes will never recur? Where, in the weak and erring temper of man, do we find a guarantee that bloodshed and crime, the fruit of other delusions, shall not again desolate the land? Let us not boast of the dignity of Reason, the victories of Science, and the golden age of taste and refinement. These are often the soil in which the worst delusions spring up and cover the land with a foliage so rank and poisonous, that the moral atmosphere is filled with pestilence and death.

As the evening advanced, the different agents in the events about to take place, were all at their posts. Strale occupied the cottage of Somers. Lyford was at Mr. Ellerson's, Somers was in attendance upon Strale, and the Water Witch, with furled sails, was resting quietly on the bosom of the river, while her vigilant crew, with a double watch, waited the orders of their master.

It was late, the same night, when Trellison left Salem for Boston. His subsequent reflections had determined him to see Governor Phips, make his confessions, and procure, if possible, a reprieve or pardon. In case of failure in his application, he could return in season to make his last effort at the scaffold. But new difficulties awaited him. Sir William was absent from town, and would not return for several days. There was no delegated authority to which application could be made, and his lady, who at the hazard of her life once saved a condemned individual, dared not and indeed could not interpose. The night was spent in anxious consultations, and ended with the conviction that his only chance of success was a public confession, and an appeal to the multitude.

CHAPTER SIXTEENTH

HARRIS, THE JAILER of Miss Lyford, we have before remarked, was extremely superstitious. The other persons on guard were nearly as much so as their superior. The characters of these men had been thoroughly studied by Strale and his friends, and they were satisfied an experiment might be made on their credulity and superstition, with reasonable hope of success. The idea very generally prevailed, that all who were active in the witch prosecutions were exposed to fiery assaults from Satan. On this account, it was deemed a religious duty to guard the prisoners with the greatest possible care, and the most resolute men were selected for this purpose.

The jailer was often apprehensive that Satan might appear in defence of his prisoners. He thought it very possible that a part of the compact might be that they should be delivered in the moment of their greatest peril. He often spoke of some probable encounter with the devil, for it was hardly possible that so faithful a servant of God should remain unmolested, while subverting the kingdom of Satan on earth. In conversation with Bolton and his associates, he often warned them to prepare for such an encounter, and told them of the best methods to beat off the Serpent, should he be so bold as to attack them. Harris thought his spiritual armor was impregnable, and his prowess irresistible, and though as yet he had no opportunity of signalizing his courage by a pitched battle with any of the demons around him, yet he boasted of one or two skirmishes in which the Adversary, though he shook his dragon head and gnashed his teeth, was finally glad to make his retreat. The courageous jailer did not use his worldly weapons, but he always confronted his enemy with passages of scripture, and, in the last resort, employed the most powerful spiritual weapon which he said never failed, and that was prayer. Harris was not much given to this exercise, for its potency, he insisted, was weakened by too frequent repetition; consequently, he kept this weapon for the last extremity, and never employed it, when other expedients would answer.

This view of Harris' character applied to Bolton and the other guards of Miss Lyford, so far as superstition was concerned, but Harris was quite their superior in other respects. He was powerful and bold, and in grappling with flesh and blood, few men could stand before him; but he was quite deceived in supposing himself a match for the imaginary demons around him. No man was more likely to make good his retreat, if he had occular demonstration of the presence of these mysterious beings.

About ten o'clock in the evening, Lyford requested the privilege of visiting his sister for the last time. He was rudely repulsed by Harris and the guard, who said they were forbidden to admit any person on any pretence whatever.

'Hitherto,' said Lyford, 'you have permitted me to visit my afflicted sister, and if she be guilty, and as much so as you allege, she is still my sister, and nature pleads in her behalf. I trust you will permit me to go in.'

'It is vain to ask,' said Harris; 'the permission you had from the Governor has been revoked, and you cannot go in.'

'Will you take no responsibility in the matter?' said Lyford, 'and let me pass for the last time?'

'None whatever,' was the reply. 'Our orders are positive, and we cannot permit you to go in.'

'Mr. Harris,' returned Lyford, 'you say my sister has made a compact with Satan; if so, I trust he will appear in her behalf; for, bad as he is, I would trust him for humanity sooner than such wretches as you. If he possesses any power, I believe he will now exert it. I was informed he was seen in the chamber of the sheriff, last night, in a threatening attitude, so that he was hardly able to proceed in his dreadful work to-day. Moreover, I am told by others, that he is excited to uncommon rage, and will not any longer tolerate the murder of his friends.'

Harris seemed startled by these remarks, and as the night was excessively dark, and the train of reflection which Lyford had awakened was not the most agreeable, the jailer began to fortify his courage by repeating passages from the Bible, and calling upon the guard to unite with him in this holy employment, assuring them that Satan would not dare to appear in the face of such rebukes as the holy scriptures contained.

'Look,' said Bolton, 'see, Mr. Harris, what terrible shape is that coming towards us?' The startled jailer cast his eyes in the direction pointed out by Bolton, and he saw, gleaming through the shade, a figure, which his terrified imagination instantly formed into that of a dragon. From his horns, streams of fire were spouting, and a sound like the hissing of a hundred serpents, rushed on the ear. A moment more, and volumes of fire poured from his mouth, discovering by their light, the hideous and distorted features of a demon, while with slow and solemn pace he advanced towards the house.

'Get thee behind me, Satan!'[1] said the agitated Harris. He then looked round for a moment, with a bewildered and uncertain gaze. Lyford had disappeared; Bolton and his companions had fled like the wind. Harris then closed his eyes, and fell on his knees, uttering a hurried and tremulous prayer. Looking up again, the fearful apparition still advanced, and when in the light that was blazing all around, Harris caught sight of his cloven foot, the unhappy jailer no longer doubted that Satan in person was at hand, in behalf of Miss Lyford. The Bible dropped from his hands; the voice of prayer died on his lips. Steel and pistol were of no avail. No other weapon remained, and taking to his heels, the unlucky Harris deserted his post, and fled like a racer for his life, into the depths of the forest. Looking for a moment from behind a tree, he saw the fiery dragon enter the house. Then, redoubling his speed, he pushed on over bushes, fences and brooks, until he plunged into a ditch, from which, after floundering about for an hour, he made shift to get, weary and exhausted, upon its neighboring bank. Even here he dared not open his eyes, lest the terrible image, in its lurid flames, should once more haunt his vision; but falling on his knees, he devoutly returned thanks, for the strength he had received to flee from the destroyer.

Meanwhile, the faithful Somers rushed into the house, and with a single stroke of his axe, broke in the door of Miss Lyford's chamber, and then bearing her down stairs, he placed her in a wagon, which had been provided at a little distance, for the occasion. Walter having divested himself of his dragon's dress, left the horns, the cloven foot and the black robe in the jailer's room, and with Lyford, hastened to the beach, where Somers and Mary had already arrived, and in a few moments, they were all safely on board the Water Witch. The wife and child of Somers had been sent on board, early in the evening, and when the next morning dawned, they were ten leagues from Salem harbor, on their way to Virginia.

The scheme which had been so completely successful was entirely the invention of Strale; its details were arranged with the utmost precision and care, and it was executed with an admirable degree of coolness and skill. Gunpowder in its various adaptations produced the fire. The burning of tobacco caused the smoke, which seemed to proceed from his breath. His face blackened and disfigured, a black gown thrown over his shoulders, and leather sandals in the form of cloven feet, completed the disguise.

It was not surprising that a device, which in ordinary circumstances would have been equally foolish and hopeless, should be, in the present state of public feeling, perfectly adapted to its end. It was then supposed that visible appearances from the world of spirits were not uncommon, and the disordered fancies of men created innumerable apparitions and shapes of evil, which the senses gifted with supernatural acuteness, were enabled to discern among the grosser forms of the material world.

The chronicle we have consulted[2] does not reveal the process by which the mode of Miss Lyford's escape was concealed from the public eye. Yet it contains some hints on this point which are reserved for our next chapter, and it also intimates that many secrets were kept by the men in power, which, had they been disclosed, would have covered the actors in these tragedies with confusion and shame, and finished at once the work of persecution and death.

CHAPTER SEVENTEENTH

THE MORNING DAWNED with a most welcome radiance upon the haggard and exhausted Harris, as he lay on the bank of a muddy brook, from which, after his desperate efforts in the ditch, he had no strength to retreat. But he soon felt the refreshing influence of the morning air, and as he cast his eye over the different and well-known objects around him, his scattered senses began to return and his courage to revive. He saw in the miserable plight of his dress and the bruises on his limbs that he had been foiled in his great battle with the adversary; but he hoped that after all Satan had been so much annoyed by his prayers and quotations, that he had fled out of the region. He dared not, however, venture back into the house, until he saw Bolton coming towards him, who having fled at the first onset, was not so stupified with terror as his friend Harris. Bolton, however, looked as if he had passed a comfortless night. He had been separated from the other guards, who had sought their own safety, and at last found shelter in a cottage, distant from town, where he remained till morning.

'How came you, Bolton, to leave me to fight the battle alone?' exclaimed Harris.

'Because, I am no match for the devil,' said Bolton; 'and you, Harris—did you stand your ground?'

'Stand it? Yes, long after you had left it, and it was not till the monster was directly upon me, that I began to retreat.'

'Retreat! you retreat?' said Bolton; 'why, you said the devil would flee at the first word you uttered. I am afraid, Harris, you are not so much of a saint as you thought.'

'Saint!' replied the indignant Harris; 'it would take an army of saints to drive off such a dragon as he who assaulted me. I tell you, Bolton, if I had not been a saint I should have been consumed by the flames that surrounded me. But thank God, I was delivered out of the mouth of the lion!'[1]

'Shall we venture into the house?' said Bolton; 'it is now clear daylight, and as dragons are abroad only in the night, I think we may go in with safety.'

'I will go,' said Harris; 'my courage revives, and methinks I could even face the dragon again. Oh! Bolton, it is a great thing to have a good conscience!'

'It is a better thing, so far as safety is concerned, to have nimble feet,' replied Bolton. 'I believe you and I, Harris, must trust more to these than to any special friendship with conscience.'

'We are both sinners, Bolton, and saints too, I hope,' said Harris; 'but look, every thing seems natural about the house; there is no mark of fire or brimstone.[2] I have faith to believe that last prayer of mine was not fruitless.'

As the jailer uttered this, they entered the door, and the first objects they saw were the horns, cloak and appurtenances of

Strale. A note was seen on the table, and Harris hastily opening it, read as follows:

'THE bird has flown. Faithful guards, what account will ye give of your stewardship? Thanks to your superstition and folly, they have given us that, which we sought in vain from your sense of justice and humanity. The wicked flee when no man pursueth.[3] If ye tremble and flee before the painted symbol of Satan, what will ye do when you meet the arch Enemy face to face?

WALTER STRALE.'

'So then we have run away from a shadow, and the devil was this Walter Strale! I thought the scoundrel was in Boston, and had given up the witch. I would as soon be hung myself, as have this thing known.'

'But it must be known,' said Bolton; 'how else can we give account of the lady's escape? We must see the magistrates, tell them the facts, and take their advice.'

'There is no other way,' returned Harris; 'it is a dreadful alternative, but I hardly think they will wish to betray us on their own account; it would cover them with disgrace as well as us.'

So saying, they proceeded to the house of one of the magistrates, who called in the sheriff and one of his assistants. After a full conference, they decided to report that the escape of Miss Lyford was effected by violence. The injury done to the door would support this view of the case, and the absence of Strale and Lyford, and the sudden departure of the Water Witch would furnish a plausible story, and allay the anger of the populace.

It was now eleven o'clock, and the population of Salem and its neighborhood, near and remote, were assembled on the hill, to witness another act in the tragedies of the times. The scaffold was overshadowed by a tree, whose graceful figure and verdant branches had long attracted the youth and maidens of the vicinity in their summer rambles, and under its pleasant shade, many a whisper of affection and many a secret of innocence and love, had been breathed to willing ears and confiding hearts.

Near this spot stood the unhappy Trellison; around and before him, and stretching away to the base of the hill, a silent and solemn multitude were waiting the arrival of the officers of the law and their hapless victim. On his right, the beautiful town was reposing in the brightness and calm of a clear summer day; but to the eye of man, a strange and startling gloom had fallen upon a scene, which up to this fatal period, had been radiant in the fairest forms of beauty and loveliness. One spot only riveted the gaze of Trellison, and as his eye explored the shaded avenue, along which the sad procession must pass, the ashy paleness of his victim's countenance, the neglected ringlets that once with magic power had played upon her neck of spotless white, and the slender figure whose graceful proportions had charmed every beholder, completely filled his imagination, and threw over his face the gloom of despair. The heavy moments rolled on, and at length the hour of twelve was announced by the under sheriff, while neither officer nor prisoner appeared. A beam of hope now lighted the eye of Trellison; he knew some unseen power had suspended or averted the fatal sentence, and with unutterable emotions, he saw the sheriff at last ascend the platform to explain the mysterious absence of the prisoner. The multitude gathered around, while the officer declared, as he said, with grief and shame inexpressible, that Miss Lyford had been withdrawn by violence; that Ringbolt and the crew of the Water Witch, in concert with Strale, had effected by stratagem and force, the escape of the criminal, and thus the law was defrauded of its demands, and the majesty of Heaven of a sacrifice, which would have done much to vindicate its insulted honor, and defeat the machinations of the devil. The people were exhorted to go home, and if any of them felt encouraged in the practice of these wicked arts, by the escape of Miss Lyford, they might be assured the law would not relax its demands, nor the officers of justice their vigilance, but the land must, at all hazards, be purged of Satan and his devices. They were also charged to pray that the mischievous and wicked maiden who had escaped, might be overtaken by the Divine vengeance, and punished for her sorceries.

At that moment, Trellison mounted the scaffold.[4] His face, which till now had worn the livid hue of death, was covered by the flush of emotion. Every eye in that immense assemblage was fixed upon him. As he flung off his cap and threw back his disordered hair, he seemed moved by an impulse little less than divine. In a few moments his aspect became composed, and in a calm and clear voice he gave utterance to the feelings which moved his inmost soul.

'Heaven, to-day, has interposed,' said this master of the assembly, 'and spared the innocent blood. Why slept thy thunders, oh Jehovah! when the dire machination entered my heart? when I cursed the innocent victim and laid snares for her life? Thou didst turn back upon my soul a tide of guilt and horror, which would have drowned me in destruction and perdition, and now thou hast checked its rage, and given me space to proclaim the innocence of that victim, whom thou hast this day saved from the altar of Moloch.[5] Hear me, magistrates and men, and ye ministers of an insulted God! hear me, old age, middle life

and youth! I proclaim in your ears that the maiden who has this
day escaped death, was guiltless of the crime for which she was
condemned to die! Deceived by my own heart, mistaking the bitter passion of revenge for zeal in the service of my Maker, it was
this hand that brought down the threatened ruin upon that child
of innocence and love. The fetters that bound me in delusion
and shame are broken for ever. But who shall wash our guilty
hands from the blood we have shed? Who shall reanimate the
cold forms that but yesterday lived and breathed in our midst?
Here, from this fatal hill, shall go down a memorial through all
departing generations, which shall brand us for ever. The winds
that sweep over these valleys and rocks shall testify against us.
Yonder tree, riven by lightning, and blasted to its very roots,
shall testify against us. This mount of offence,[6] on which we now
stand, shall testify against us. For me, I go from this place, to
solitude, penitence and prayer. Go you to the like solemn offices, and bless your Maker, as I do, that this vial of wrath has
been stayed.[7] Hold back your hands from blood; already it cries
for vengeance from the ground.[8] Be grateful, as I am, that we are
not yet pursued by his avenging hand, or smitten by the thunders of his wrath.'

The speaker descended from the scaffold. As he passed
through the spell-bound and awe-struck multitude, no one mo-
lested him. He lingered for a moment on the edge of the forest, and then waving his hand, as if he would again impress the
solemn truths he had uttered, on the minds of the audience, he
disappeared among the tress. An unbroken silence reigned for a
few moments through all that vast assembly, and the first words
that were spoken, were an expression of thankfulness that the
innocent maiden had escaped; but the solemn impressions of

the day failed to arrest the mighty torrent of superstition that was now rushing over the land. There were not wanting those who attributed this change in Trellison to the power of her magic arts. This belief gained ground, as Trellison was never more seen in public, and his retreat was undiscovered and unknown. The delusion still prevailed; other scenes of blood were witnessed; and history, faithful to its trust, has branded that age and its men of power and influence with an infamy which must abide upon them for ever.

CHAPTER EIGHTEENTH

THE WATER WITCH glided on her way with fine breezes and in gallant trim, as if conscious of her beauty and the charm she spread over the waters. In truth, this gem of the ocean was a sort of idol with Capt. Ringbolt, who declared he could never survive her loss. He insisted that her like had never before floated on the sea, and that when her day of service was over, old Neptune would give her a tomb in some bed of coral and pearls, and send up a pillar of foam in perpetual commemoration of this graceful jewel in his crown. Her passengers, however, were occupied with far graver thoughts. The first interview between Strale and Mary was too simple and impressive to be here described. It is enough to say, that a remembrance of the dangers and distresses of the last few months, while it bound them to each other by the strongest ties, led them also to united and devout thanksgivings to that divine Being who had preserved them through all.

The voyage to Virginia was soon accomplished. Capt. Ringbolt, whose kind offices were so essential to the safety of Miss Lyford, and without whose agency the project for her deliverance must have failed, was well rewarded for his services. It is but just to say, however, that his humanity and generosity prompted him to assist in the undertaking without any stipulated recompense. He had no fear that his trade would be essentially disturbed, as he was confident a state of things so unnatural must soon pass away. Yet for a time he thought it prudent to keep up his traffic along the southern coast, where his business might still be prosecuted with success.

A few days after the arrival of the party at Virginia, they found a vessel for England, in which they determined to embark. Having established Somers in a small house, and furnished him with means to cultivate a good farm, Walter and Lyford, with Mary, sailed for Europe. The voyage was prosperous, and in two months from their embarkation they reached the shores of France, and soon entered its gay metropolis, where in the family of Mr. Strale, Mary Lyford found the affection of parents, and gave in return the love and gratitude of a child. All the scenes of their past history were related by Walter, and in a few weeks, with the full consent of his parents, he led Mary to the nuptial altar. Their happiness was now complete. Years of love and tranquillity glided away, untarnished by the lapse of time, consecrated by a visible communion with God, and the life of christian faith.

The same enlightened and devoted piety which resisted the force of the wildest superstition, was equally victorious over the gayeties and follies of Paris. They were placed in circumstances where the attractions of the world, its distinctions and honors, were freely offered them; but they chose to live as pilgrims and strangers on the earth, looking for a better country, even a heavenly. After a few years' residence in Paris, they removed to Bremen, the original home of Mr. Strale, where Walter, highly distinguished for his literary character, filled one of the most

important civil offices, and diffused around him the best influences of the christian faith, adorned and supported by a truly
christian example.

Mr. Lyford returned to New England. He loved the land of the
pilgrims; and notwithstanding its follies and crimes, it was still
the home of his heart. He had seen among the friends of his sister one whom his judgment not less than his fancy recommended
to his affections. It was his first, his long cherished, and ever
constant love. On his arrival at Virginia he addressed a letter to
Miss Elliott, in which he disclosed his attachment, and begged
she would reciprocate a love which could be none but hers. This
communication was not wholly unexpected; for their early sympathies, and the high esteem in which Lyford had ever been held,
had long before this awakened responsive affection in her own
heart. Soon after, he appeared in Boston, and was united in mar-
riage to one who was the pride of her family, and whose charms of
person and manners were only excelled by those of Miss Lyford.

It was one of the first objects of Lyford on his return to New
England, to seek the unhappy Trellison, and convey to him the
free forgiveness of his sister, and her sincere desires for his usefulness and happiness here and hereafter. He was particularly
charged by Mary to perform this act of christian charity; for the
letter of Trellison, which she read on board the Water Witch,
made a deep impression on her mind. She well knew the gloomy
fanaticism of his temper, and was anxious to mitigate as far as
possible, the anguish and horror which had overwhelmed him.
Bitterness and revenge had no abode in the bosom of Miss Lyford;
and though she had previously written to Trellison and assured
him of her forgiveness, she was not satisfied till she could know
from her brother that her message had been communicated.

Lyford had much difficulty in ascertaining the residence of Trellison. He found him at last in a remote settlement, where he was devoting his time to the instruction of children, and exerting the best influence in the very small and scattered community in which he lived. They conversed together of the scenes through which they had passed; in which Trellison declared that so far as he was an actor, he could never forgive himself; and his only hope of pardon from Heaven was founded on the assurance of forgiveness to the chief of sinners.[1]

———

The ancient chronicle from which we have sketched these pictures here drops its curtain. We find no further traces of the different individuals whose characters and doings have flitted like a dream before our minds. But their history shadows forth their destiny; and we may trace its brighter or darker lines, by the characters in which they have been seen.

That memorable tree under which these deeds of terror were done, was then in its greenness and beauty. Not long after, and it literally fulfilled the prophetic intimation of Trellison. "Smitten, as was supposed by lightning, it withered away, and stood for years with leafless, outstretched arms, and sapless trunk, until burned to the ground, by the descendants of the third and fourth generation of those who suffered under it. In superstitious minds, tempests and torrents could not wash away the blood from the unhallowed hill whereon it grew, and the soil was cursed and barren of wholesome vegetation."*[2]

———

* 'Historical Letters,' by A. CUSHING, Esq.

True Religion[3] acknowledges no affinity with superstition. She has indeed suffered from the artificial bonds in which skepticism has entwined them; but if her robes have been soiled and her countenance marred by the unnatural position she is thus compelled to occupy, her voice of charity and accents of love still proclaim her divine, and she will always come forth with renovated beauty, and offer to man the best antidote against superstition, and his only true happiness for time and eternity.

Publication History of *The Salem Belle*

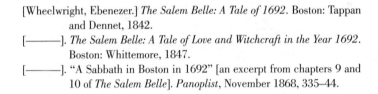

[Wheelwright, Ebenezer.] *The Salem Belle: A Tale of 1692*. Boston: Tappan
    and Dennet, 1842.
[————]. *The Salem Belle: A Tale of Love and Witchcraft in the Year 1692*.
    Boston: Whittemore, 1847.
[————]. "A Sabbath in Boston in 1692" [an excerpt from chapters 9 and
    10 of *The Salem Belle*]. *Panoplist*, November 1868, 335–44.

APPENDIX B:
Reviews of *The Salem Belle*

Reviews of *The Salem Belle: A Tale of 1692*
[by Ebenezer Wheelwright]

Unsigned review of *The Salem Belle*, *Boston Daily Courier*, November 30,
1842, [2].

    Tappan & Dennet have published a little work, with this title, being the
material circumstances of a remarkable legend, founded on the singular
events of 1692, or the days of Witchcraft in Salem.

Unsigned review of *The Salem Belle*, *Bay State Democrat*, December 1,
1842, [2].

    Tappan & Dennet have published a little work with this title, being the
material circumstances of a remarkable legend, founded on the singular
events of 1692, or the days of Witchcraft in Salem. The reputation of those
days has, we are well persuaded, cast too deep a shade on the memories of
our forefathers. A careful investigation into the history of the times will show
that the witchcraft delusion was but an engine set in motion by priestcraft, to
destroy its opponents. How far this volume goes towards setting the matter

in its true light, we are unable to say; it is, however, worthy of attention, and has the appearance of an attractive tale.

Unsigned review of *The Salem Belle*, *Boston Evening Mercantile Journal*, December 1, 1842, [2].

This is a Tale of 1692, published in a neat volume, by Tappan & Dennet, of this city. The scene is laid in Salem, in the days of witchcraft, and it gives a graphic and interesting view of the state of society at that period when Delusion spread her thick mists over New England.

Unsigned review of *The Salem Belle*, *Daily Atlas* (Boston), December 1, 1842, [2].

Messrs. Tappan & Dennet, 114 Washington Street, have published, in a neat little volume, a tale of 1692, the era of Salem Witchcraft, with the above title. We have not had time to examine its merits, but its subject is one of deep interest and well adapted to supply the materials of romance.

Unsigned review of *The Salem Belle*, *Boston Daily Evening Transcript*, December 2, 1842, [2]. Reprinted in the *Newburyport Herald*, December 5, 1842, [2] and December 6, 1842, [2].

This is a tale of old Salem witchcraft, embodying a remarkable legend of the year 1692, and presenting in the main, an interesting story of the olden time. The belle, herself, though not one of the ancient witches, was a bewitching creature, and married without "witchcraft" to a lover who, unlike Othello, had shared with her many a perilous adventure. The book has a sober moral, showing that true religion has no affinity with superstition and skepticism.

Unsigned review of *The Salem Belle*, *Boston Evening Gazette*, December 2, 1842, [3].

From the same publishers [as those of *Robinson Crusoe*, Tappan and Dennet] we have also received, a volume of 238 pages with the annexed title, purporting to be a Tale of 1692. It contains eighteen chapters—but we have not had time to peruse any of them.

Unsigned review of *The Salem Belle*, *Salem Gazette*, December 2, 1842, [2].

This is the title of one of TAPPAN & DENNET'S neat, little publications, from the press of S. N. Dickinson—It contains, it is said, all the material circumstances of a remarkable legend, founded on the singular events of 1692. It is the object of the tale to hold up the beacons of the past, and in this connection to illustrate the social conditions, the habits, manners, and general state of New England, in these early days of its history. The author justly remarks: "Our fathers were not faultless, but [as] a community, a nobler race was never seen on the globe: they were indeed in some degree superstitious and intolerant, but far less so than even the brilliant circles of wealth and fashion, they left behind, in their father land; and it will be well for their sons, if they do not stumble over worse delusions and fall into more fatal errors, than those of their primitive ancestors." The tale appears to be well wrought up, independently of its local interest, which ought to commend for it a ready sale in this vicinity. For our copy we are indebted to Mr. J. P. JEWETT.

Unsigned review of *The Salem Belle*, *Salem Observer*, December 3, 1842, [2].

Our thanks are due to the publishers, Tappan & Dennet, for a beautifully printed volume, bearing this title. It is, as its title imports, a tale founded on "the material circumstances of a remarkable legend, founded on the singular events of 1692," the period in which the witchcraft delusion was in full tide of operation. The author, in an interesting style, introduces new scenes and hitherto unknown actors in that fatal tragedy, which so deeply stains the history of New England. As a specimen of the work, we give the following description of a successful plan, by her brother and lover, to release Miss Lyford who had been arrested and thrown into prison on charge of witchcraft.

[A lengthy excerpt appears, from pages 214 to 221 in the first edition. The same excerpt appears from pages 165 to 169 in the present text.]

The work is for sale by W. & S. B. Ives, through whom we have received a copy.

Unsigned review of *The Salem Belle*, *Boston Post*, December 5, 1842, [1]. Reprinted in *Boston Statesman*, December 10, 1842, [4].

We have perused this book as closely as its inordinate dullness would allow. And although it is so very common-place that even its faults are not at once perceptible, yet on minute inspection it seems one of the most *verdant* stories it was ever our ill luck to read. The scene is laid in Boston and Salem, at the period of the Salem witchcraft. Boston is described as possessing *one* wharf, *thirty* sail of vessels, and as being composed of *eight hundred* houses, but in the next breath the hero is conducted to his "hotel"—a *hotel* in the times of the Puritans. Again, the characters talk just as they do now-a-days, and, with the exception of some set description and the witches, one would never discover that he was not reading a tale of 1842. We never knew before that the term "rowdies" was used in 1692, however many there might be deserving of the name. In a word, the whole thing is a humdrum failure—the trickeries of the bewitched—the behaviour of the supposed witches—and even the accusation and condemnation of the heroine herself, are told without the least power. The story wanders here and there without object, and finally winds up like a nursery tale. We would advise the writer to study well the art of novel writing ere another attempt. We were vexed at having wasted our time over such a hodge podge of stuff, developing little or no talent and less tact.

Unsigned review of *The Salem Belle*, *Salem Register*, December 5, 1842, [2]. Quoted review from *Boston Evening Bulletin*.

We are indebted to the author for a copy of this excellent little book, which may be obtained of F. PUTNAM, Essex Street, and will serve admirably for a Christmas or New Year's present. The editor of the *Boston Evening Bulletin*, who is something of a *connoisseur* in such matters, thus speaks of the "BELLE":—

THE SALEM BELLE.—This is a neat little work in one volume, of 238 pages, which is published by Messrs. Tappan and Dennet, 114 Washington street. It is a tale founded on the singular events of 1692, when Witchcraft, like other popular delusions of the present day, destroyed the peace and happiness of many families. The author remarks, that it is too late to revive the folly of witchcraft, but other follies are pressing on the community— fanaticism in various ways is moulding the public feeling into unnatural shapes and shadowing forth a train of undefined evils, whose forms of mischief are yet to be developed. In this state of things, our true wisdom is to take counsel of the past, and not suffer ourselves to be led astray by bold and startling theories, which can only waste the mental energies, and make shipwreck of the mind itself on some fatal rock of superstition or infidelity.—The *Salem Belle* is a simple and beautiful tale, and is beautifully written. The characters are well portrayed, and that of Mary Graham is sweetly drawn. We cheerfully commend this work to our readers.

Unsigned review of *The Salem Belle*, *New York Daily Tribune*, December 6, 1842, [1].

This is the title of a small, neat volume, containing a tale, designed to illustrate the social habits and manners of the people of New-England during the days of the Salem Witchcraft. The attempt, we believe, has never before been made; though there is evidently scope for the most interesting and valuable exercise of the novelist's power. The style of this little book is easy and graceful, and the incidents of the tale possesses [possess] variety and no little interest.

Unsigned review of *The Salem Belle*, *New-York Evangelist*, December 8, 1842, 192. Reprinted also in the Quarto Edition, December 8, 1842, 388.

We must say we have read this book with pain and dislike. Its scene is laid at Salem and Boston, and is connected with what in this country is called the "Salem witchcraft." And while there are some things in it clearly good, we were sorry to see the stern and rigid piety of the Pilgrims *unnecessarily* stigmatized, in the persons of its most prominent early defenders. It is enough for the skeptic, and those who have *forsaken* the Puritan faith, to exhume the faults of the dead, while one who like this author seems to have correct views of religious faith, should suffer them to sleep. There are many, who either in ignorance or wickedness, seem to identify the religion of the Puritans with witchcraft, as though they alone of all the earth, believed in those dreadful dogmas. We often hear of the "Salem witchcraft"—why do we not also hear of "witchcraft" at Yarmouth, and Chelmsford, and Cambridge, and Huntingdon, in England[?] Those writers who directly or indirectly would stigmatize the faith of the Puritans, never tell us that other men believed and acted in like manner. They can vilify the memory of the Puritans, and of Cotton Mather in particular, as the "chief cause, agent, believer, and justifier," of the persecutions of that day. But we *deny* the charge, and call them slanderers of the dead that utter it. They do not tell us that Blackstone, Sir Matthew Hale, Sir Thomas Browne, Chief Justice Holt, William Penn, and others of the same class of honored names, believed in witchcraft, and condemned the victims to death. To say that Blackstone or William Penn believed in witches, would bring no odium upon the Christian faith of the Puritans, and so there is no occasion for saying it!

The men of that day had their errors, and great errors, but they were not alone in their peculiarities. And neither this writer of duodecimos, nor that "eminent historian of Harvard College," will be able "to brand that age and its men of power and influence with an infamy which must abide upon them forever." If they erred, they erred in common with all the rest of the world, and the religious and civil institutions they have left us, cast a glory about their names, that will forever obscure their defects, and make brighter and brighter still, their noble virtues.

We do not wish to say the writer of the book before us, wished to bring odium on the names of our Fathers; indeed, we do not think so, but such will be the effect of it. And we cannot see any sufficient reason to justify it; nor we do not think that the author has, as he professes in his introduction, illustrated truly "the social condition, habits, manners and general state of New-England, in the early days of its history."

Unsigned review of *The Salem Belle*, *American Traveller*, December 9, 1842, [2].

    The Salem Belle.—Messrs. Tappan & Dennet have published, in their usual handsome style, a 12 mo. volume, under the above title. It is founded upon the terrible tragedy of 1691, when the whole community, urged on by a weak and vindictive minister of Salem, and a most credulous one of Boston, went mad upon a subject now exploded, but then of fearful import, and which filled the island with consternation—and deluged some of its fairest portions with blood.

    This story is well and movingly told, and presents the whole horror of the time in that strong and true light, which can only be done with a masterly hand. We consider it the duty of the community to possess themselves fully with the history of past delusions, in order more effectively to guard against the many to which the times are periodically exposed. That whole nations like individuals may run mad, is peculiarly true of the Anglo-Saxon race,— and the history of past excesses will prove the strongest guard for the future. It is happy when the knowledge can be obtained with pleasure, as well as profit, as in this instance. The lovers of a well told tale will find a rich feast in The Salem Belle.

Unsigned review of *The Salem Belle*, *New England Puritan*, December 9, 1842, [2].

    If parents wish their children to acquire a taste for novel reading, so that they may be ready to devour every fictitious work that comes in their way, with all the poison it may contain, this is a good work for them to commence with. The moral bearings of the work are just enough to exclude all qualms of conscience, and give it the completest influence in the formation of such a taste.

Unsigned review of *The Salem Belle*, *Albany Evening Journal*, December 16, 1842, [2].

    This, as its title imports, is a story founded upon the strange delusion which in 1692 stained the soil of Massachusetts with so much innocent blood. The tale is made up of veritable incidents and brings upon the stage new scenes and hitherto unknown actions in that fatal tragedy—There are delusions almost as lamentable as that of the Salem Witchcraft which still linger in the land, and it is by way of antidote to such poison that the volume in question is offered to the public.

Unsigned review of *The Salem Belle*, *Boston Recorder*, December 30, 1842, 206.

We have read this story with much interest. It is an exciting tale of witch-craft times, and is written in an elegant and captivating style. It exhibits, no doubt faithfully, the social condition, the habits, manners, piety, and super-stition of the early days of New England. But we cannot help thinking that it bears too severely upon the motives of some of the eminent divines—Cotton Mather in particular—who were subjects of that dreadful witchcraft delu-sion, and who were active promoters of the shocking measures which were instituted in their imagined conflict with Satan. The impression which the author of this tale leaves upon the reader's mind is, that the witchcraft delu-sion was rather an artifice of wicked men, and that its main evils were the result of diabolical frauds, in which some of the clergy were but too easily duped and led to participate. The "Salem Belle," the heroine of the tale, was a victim to private malice and revenge, charged by a discarded lover with witchcraft, and brought, with most unnatural rapidity, to conviction and sentence of death—from which sentence she, however, escapes by the romantic aid of her accepted lover, and flees to Virginia. We are aware that the true history of Salem Witchcraft has not yet been written; but we are not prepared to believe, that its real characteristics are developed in the narra-tive of the "Salem Belle."

[James Russell Lowell], review of *The Salem Belle*, *Pioneer*, January 1843, 44.

This little novel is, we are informed, the production of a young merchant of this city, whose first attempt in the art of book-making it appears to be. It is disfigured by several strange anachronisms, not the least remarkable of which, are the introduction of lightning conductors some twenty or thirty years prior to the birth of Franklin, and of a Virginian negro slave, who, nearly a century before the Declaration of American Independence, "pro-fessed to be a thorough democrat, and insisted that all men were born free and equal." These, however, do not probably mar the interest of the book to the general reader.

The story is one of love, and is pleasingly told. The main interest turns upon the famous witchcraft delusion of 1692, and the danger incurred by the heroine, who becomes involved in the persecution levelled at every one suspected of dealing in the black art, and is rescued by her lover, and carried off to Virginia, on the day previous to that appointed for her death on the scaffold.

Unsigned review of *The Salem Belle*, *Artist: A Monthly Lady's Book*, January 1843, 239.

This tale is intended to elucidate the delusion under which persons suspected of witchcraft were persecuted about the close of the 17th century.—The story is well told, and possesses great interest. A highly religious feeling pervades the whole volume.

Unsigned review of *The Salem Belle*, *Knickerbocker*, January 1843, 102.

'THE SALEM BELLE,' a tale of 1692, comes to us in a neat and tasteful volume from the press of Messrs. TAPPAN AND DENNET, Boston. It is an agreeable and entertaining, but not particularly powerful story, connected with that famous delusion which has made Salem a place so renowned for 'imaginary' persons. It is the object of the work to 'hold up the beacons of the past, and in this connection to illustrate the social condition, habits, manners, and general state of New-England, in those early days of its history.' We believe with the author, that at a time when fanaticism in various ways is moulding the public feeling into unnatural shapes, and shadowing forth a train of undefined evils, a work which shall serve to guard the public mind against a recurrence of popular delusions will supply an important desideratum among the books of the day, in 'making many' of which verily there seems to be 'no end.'

Unsigned review of *The Salem Belle*, *Merchants' Magazine and Commercial Review*, January 1, 1843, 104.

Interwoven in a rather attractive and exciting tale, we have recorded the events connected with the Salem witchcraft delusion that prevailed near the close of the seventeenth century. The elements of delusion always exist in the human mind. Sometimes they slumber for years, and then break forth with volcanic energy spreading ruin and desolation in their path. "Even now, the distant roar of these terrible agents comes with confused and ominous sound on the ear. What form of mischief they will assume, is among the mysteries of the future; that desolation will follow in their train, no one can doubt; that they will purify the moral atmosphere, and throw up mighty land-marks as guides to future ages, is equally certain. The evil or good which shall be the final result, depends, under Providence, on the measures of wisdom we may gather from the lessons of the past." It appears to be the design of these pages to hold up the beacons of the past, and, in this connection, to illustrate the sound [social] condition, the habits, manners, and general state of New England in those early days of its history.

Henry T. Tuckerman, review of *The Salem Belle*, *Boston Miscellany of Literature*, February 1843, 94.

This little story possesses some local interest. It is from an anonymous source. The object of the author is to illustrate the extraordinary delusion which resulted in the sacrifice of so many victims of popular superstition, under the name of witches. The period to which the tale refers, abounds in materials for the novelist, and, in judicious and gifted hands, might be rendered fearfully interesting. The present attempt is of a more humble order, and contains some evidences of want of practice or ability in the author. To those, however, who find amusement in such fictions, it will afford entertainment. In the preface it is justly observed that "the elements of delusion always exist in the human mind." The simple narrative of "Salem Witchcraft," however, (as related, for instance, by Upham), appears to us, far more impressive, than any but a truly powerful delineation of the subject, in the form of a drama, romance or tale.

Unsigned review of *The Salem Belle*, *Sargent's New Monthly Magazine*, February 1843, 95–96.

An interesting tale founded on a remarkable New England legend of 1692. The horrors of the popular delusion, which swept like a pestilence over our land, are pictured in glowing colors; and the serene influence of true religion upon the mind is strongly contrasted with the exciting effects of superstition. The closing chapters of the book are calculated to awaken a deep, and sometimes thrilling interest. The style throughout is unaffected and agreeable, but, as is usually the case with first productions, it is somewhat wanting in terseness and vigor. The author says in his preface, "It is the object of the following pages to hold up the beacons of the past, and in this connection to illustrate the social condition, the habits, manners, and general state of New England in these early days of its history. We love to contemplate the piety and simplicity, while we deplore the superstition of those times."

Reviews of *The Salem Belle: A Tale of Love and Witchcraft*
in the Year 1692 [by Ebenezer Wheelwright]

Unsigned review of *The Salem Belle*, *Boston Recorder*, July 22, 1847,
115–16.

This pleasant tale was written with the design of showing the danger of
popular delusions, and guarding the public mind against their recurrence.
Descriptions of the social conditions and early habits and manners of New
England, as well as notices of well known localities, will render this volume
an agreeable one to the New England reader.

Unsigned review of *The Salem Belle*, *Salem Register*, July 22, 1847, [2].

Messrs. W. & S. B. Ives, 232 Essex street, have for sale a new edition of
The Salem Belle, a tale of Love and Witchcraft, in the year 1692—recently
published by John M. Whittemore, Boston. It makes a neat little volume of
238 pages.

Unsigned review of *The Salem Belle*, *Boston Recorder*, July 29, 1847, 118.

THE SALEM BELLE.—Such is the very inappropriate title, as we think,
of a small volume, giving some recent account of the superstitious and affecting incidents connected with the "Salem witchcraft." It has its uses and
attractions, and will find plenty of readers. Printed by J. M. Whittemore 114
Washington street.

APPENDIX C:
Scholarship on, and Scholarly Mention of,
The Salem Belle

———————

Bell, Michael Davitt. *Hawthorne and the Historical Romance of New Eng-
    land*. Princeton: Princeton University Press, 1971.
Bercovitch, Sacvan. *The Office of "The Scarlet Letter."* Baltimore: Johns
    Hopkins University Press, 1991.
Kopley, Richard. "Adventures with Poe and Hawthorne." *Edgar Allan Poe
    Review* 14, no. 1 (2013): 16–35.

———. "The Missing Man of *The Scarlet Letter*." In *Nathaniel Hawthorne in the College Classroom*, edited by Christopher Diller and Sam Coale, 13–23. New York: AMS Press, 2015.

———. *The Threads of "The Scarlet Letter": A Study of Hawthorne's Transformative Art*. Newark: University of Delaware Press, 2003.

Orians, G. Harrison. "The Angel of Hadley in Fiction: A Study of the Sources of Hawthorne's 'The Grey Champion.'" *American Literature* 4 (1932): 257–69.

———. "New England Witchcraft in Fiction." *American Literature* 2 (1930): 54–71.

Schwab, Gabriele. "Seduced by Witches: Nathaniel Hawthorne's *The Scarlet Letter* in the Context of New England Witchcraft Fictions." In *Seduction and Theory: Readings of Gender, Representation, and Rhetoric*, edited by Dianne Hunter, 170–91. Urbana: University of Illinois Press, 1989.

Smith, Nolan E. "Author-Identification for Six Wright I Titles: Cleveland and Doughty." *Papers of the Bibliographical Society of America* 65 (1971): 173–74.

NOTES

Introduction

1. Isaac G. Reed to Mary Reed, January 26, 1843, Reed Family Papers, Rare Book and Manuscript Library, Columbia University, New York.
2. The nursery rhyme is

Jack Sprat could eat no fat,
    His wife could eat no lean,
And so between them both, you see,
    They licked the platter clean.

For further information, see Iona Opie and Peter Opie, eds., *The Oxford Dictionary of Nursery Rhymes*, 2nd ed. (Oxford: Oxford University Press, 1997), 279–80. For the biblical phrase "the sons of Anak," see Numbers 13:33. Herman Melville refers to the great squid as "the Anak of the tribe" of cuttlefish in *Moby-Dick*. See *The Writings of Herman Melville*, 14 vols. (Evanston: Northwestern University Press/Newberry Library, 1988), 6:277. He also refers to William Shakespeare's contemporaries Christopher Marlowe, John Webster, John Ford, Francis Beaumont, and Ben Jonson as "those Anaks of men" in "Hawthorne and His Mosses" (9:252–53).

3. I. Reed to M. Reed, January 26, 1843, Reed Family Papers.
4. These page numbers come from this volume of *The Salem Belle*.
5. [Ebenezer Wheelwright], *The Salem Belle* (Boston: Tappan and Dennet, 1842), title page. Courtesy of Lilly Library, Indiana University, Bloomington, Indiana.
6. Sarah R. Derby to Mary Reed, October 13, 1841, Reed Family Papers.
7. *Stimpson's Boston Directory* (Boston: Stimpson, 1841), 461; *Stimpson's Boston Directory* (Boston: Stimpson, 1842), 490.
8. *Salem Belle* (1842), copy 1, Clark ADD 423, C. E. Frazer Clark Collection, Phillips Library, Peabody Essex Museum, Salem, Mass. I

am grateful to the Phillips Library for permission to publish this inscription.

9. [Ebenezer Wheelwright], *Traditions of Palestine; or, Scenes in the Holy Land in the Days of Christ* (Boston: Graves and Young, 1863). Wheelwright acknowledged his authorship in a letter to John A. Vinton on October 10, 1867, one held in the New England Historical and Genealogical Society in Boston, Mass. (SG VIN 6, Vinton Collection). For further information on Wheelwright and his writing, see "A Novel by Ebenezer Wheelwright," in my *The Threads of "The Scarlet Letter"* (Newark: University of Delaware Press, 2003), 64–96. See also my essay "Adventures with Poe and Hawthorne," *Edgar Allan Poe Review* 14, no. 1 (2013), 16–35 (esp. 23–33); and "The Missing Man of *The Scarlet Letter*," *Nathaniel Hawthorne in the College Classroom*, ed. Christopher Diller and Sam Coale (New York: AMS Press, 2015), 13–23.

10. Some of this biographical material may be found in Kopley, *Threads*. For the focus on Santo Domingo, see "Death of Eben Wheelwright," *Boston Daily Globe*, June 12, 1877, [3]; and ["Mr. Ebenezer Wheelwright"], *Boston Daily Advertiser*, June 12, 1877, [1]. For the amount of Wheelwright's debt at the time of his bankruptcy, see "Petition by Debtor for Benefit of the Act of Congress," March 5, 1842, file 730, RG 21, National Archives and Records Administration, Northeast Region (Waltham, Mass.). For the final credit rating, see "Massachusetts, R. G. Dun and Company Credit Report Volumes," Baker Library, Harvard Business School, 2:665. For permission to cite this final credit rating, I am grateful to the Baker Library Historical Collections. Ebenezer Wheelwright's wife was Sarah Boddily; their children were Henry Blatchford, Sarah, and Mary Abney. (See Wheelwright to Vinton, October 10, 1867, Vinton Collection.)

11. For the comment on his "integrity" and "credulity," see "Mr. Ebenezer Wheelwright, Aged 77," *Newburyport Daily Herald*, June 13, 1877, [3].

12. For Wheelwright as a "pillar in the church," see the unsigned obituary in the *Congregationalist and Boston Recorder*, June 13, 1877, 188. The editor of the newspaper was Henry M. Dexter. Information on Wheelwright's editing the *Panoplist* is available in Kopley, *Threads*, 70. The *Panoplist* and the *Congregationalist* are available at the Congregational Library in Boston. The article about the evangelical preaching of Charles G. Finney, "A Solemn Scene in the Ministry of Mr. Finney," by "Eben

Wheelwright," appeared in the *Congregationalist and Boston Recorder*, October 4, 1876, 313, and was reprinted, without its second paragraph, as "Mr. Finney in a Moment of Peril," in *Worth Keeping: Selected from "The Congregationalist and Boston Recorder," 1870–1879* (Boston: Greene, 1880), 245–49. The name "Eben Wheelwright" appears in the "Contents" of the book (8). An advertisement for this book, with Wheelwright's name and contribution, appears in the *Congregationalist* from December 17, 1879, through May 12, 1880. *Worth Keeping* was included in the exhibition The Grolier Club Collects II and is included in the exhibition catalog. (For a recent appreciation of Finney, see Marilynne Robinson, "Who Was Oberlin?," in *When I Was a Child I Read Books* [2012; repr., New York: Picador, 2013], 165–81 [esp. 170–71].) Other pieces by Wheelwright in the *Congregationalist* are "Voices of the Years" (August 26, 1875, 265), "Methods of Revival Work" (May 10, 1876, 146), and "Reading Hymns" (November 1, 1876, 346).

13. With the phrase "beneath the American Renaissance," I allude to David S. Reynolds's great monograph, *Beneath the American Renaissance: The Subversive Imagination in the Age of Emerson and Melville* (New York: Knopf, 1988). Harold K. Bush is planning an edited collection, in the tradition of *Beneath the American Renaissance*, titled "Above the American Renaissance."

14. I have not yet determined the identity of "J. N. L."

15. For the argument that social conflict within Salem Village was the critical context, see Paul Boyer and Stephen Nissenbaum, *Salem Possessed: The Social Origins of Witchcraft* (Cambridge, Mass.: Harvard University Press, 1974). For the contention that the devastating Second Indian War in Maine was that context, see Mary Beth Norton, *In the Devil's Snare: The Salem Witchcraft Crisis of 1692* (New York: Knopf, 2002).

16. For a study of the afterlife of the Salem witchcraft delusion prior to the twentieth century, see Gretchen A. Adams's *The Specter of Salem: Remembering the Witch Trials in Nineteenth-Century America* (Chicago: University of Chicago Press, 2008). For her consideration of the Salem witchcraft period and American literature (but not including *The Salem Belle*), see pp. 62–63 and 182–83.

17. According to Genealogical Notes, Wheelwright Family Papers, Massachusetts Historical Society, Boston, "Wheelwright espoused early the anti-slavery cause and wrote frequently on its behalf" (35–36).

I am grateful to the Massachusetts Historical Society for permission to quote this material. After the Civil War, Wheelwright continued to be actively antislavery: he wrote to a fellow editor in 1868 about the magazine he edited, "The 'Panoplist' is thoroughly antislavery." See Wheelwright to unidentified editor, March 21, 1868, BR box 120 (38), Huntington Library, San Marino, Calif. This item is reproduced by permission of the Huntington Library.

18. For further information on Mary Moody Emerson, consult Phyllis Cole's fine study *Mary Moody Emerson and the Origins of Transcendentalism: A Family History* (New York: Oxford University Press, 1998). Sandra Petrulionis and Noelle Baker are now working on an NEH-supported digital edition of Mary Moody Emerson's almanacs. We may also see an affinity between Wheelwright's Christian thematic and that of Harriet Beecher Stowe.

19. See Ralph Waldo Emerson, *The Collected Works of Ralph Waldo Emerson*, ed. Alfred R. Ferguson et al., 10 vols. (Cambridge, Mass.: Harvard University Press, 1971–2013), 2:77–78.

20. Wheelwright, "A Sabbath in Boston in 1692," *Panoplist* 2, no. 11 (1868): 335–44. Notably, earlier issues of the *Panoplist* featured, on the inside front wrapper, advertisements for the third edition of *Traditions of Palestine* (vol. 2, nos. 2–10 [February to October 1868]).

21. For a fuller treatment of the reviews, see Kopley, *Threads*, 75–82.

22. See [Ebenezer Wheelwright], *The Salem Belle: A Tale of Love and Witchcraft in the Year 1692* (Boston: Whittemore, 1847).

23. See my summary of inscriptions in *The Salem Belle* in *Threads*, 145–46. One inscription from mother to daughter was "Harriet C. Spooner. / from her mother / 1843." This item is reproduced by permission of the Huntington Library. A second such inscription was "Abby Sanford / from / her Mother / Jan. 1845" (Special Collections and Archives, Kent State University Libraries). I am grateful to Kent State University Libraries for permission to use this inscription. An inscription from friend to friend was "Presented To Mariah / By a Friend" (University of South Florida Library).

24. "The Hall of Fantasy" appeared in the February 1843 issue of the *Pioneer* (49–55) and "The Birth-Mark" in the March 1843 issue (113–19).

25. That Hawthorne could have received the book in October 1842 is indicated by the date of the inscription to Hannah Gould in a copy of *The Salem Belle* held by the Phillips Library of the Peabody Essex Museum

(see note 8). That Hawthorne visited Boston in late October 1842 is clear from his November 8, 1842, notebook entry, "Since the last date [October 10, 1842], we [his wife, Sophia, and he himself] have paid a visit of nine days to Boston and Salem, whence we returned a week ago yesterday." I cite Nathaniel Hawthorne, *The American Notebooks*, vol. 8 of *The Centenary Edition of the Works of Nathaniel Hawthorne*, ed. William Charvat, 23 vols. (Columbus: Ohio State University Press, 1962–94), 363. For the comment about Hawthorne's being given books, see Julian Hawthorne, *Hawthorne Reading: An Essay* (Cleveland: Rowfant Club, 1902), 117. For the comment about Hawthorne's reading later-forgotten novels, see Julian Hawthorne, *Nathaniel Hawthorne and His Wife: A Biography*, 2nd ed., 2 vols. (Boston: Osgood, 1885), 1:125.

26. I first presented the parallels between three passages in *The Salem Belle* and three passages in *The Scarlet Letter* in *Threads*, 84–89.

27. Nathaniel Hawthorne, *The Scarlet Letter*, vol. 1 of Charvat, *Centenary Edition Works*.

28. Brandon Schrand has pointed out (in an e-mail to the author, June 3, 2005) that the name "Captain Ringbolt" was taken as a pseudonym by Wheelwright's nephew John Codman, who dedicated his *Sailors' Life and Sailors' Yarns* (New York: Francis, 1847) to Wheelwright's father, Codman's own grandfather, Ebenezer Wheelwright Sr. (Our Ebenezer Wheelwright was Ebenezer Wheelwright Jr.) Codman's book was reviewed by Herman Melville—see *Writings of Herman Melville*, 9:205–11. John Codman was the son of Ebenezer Wheelwright's oldest sister, Mary, and her husband, also named John Codman. Other siblings of Ebenezer Wheelwright's were older sisters Jane and Ann; his older brother, William, and William's twin, Elizabeth; Ebenezer's younger brothers Isaac and Abraham; and younger sister Susanna. Jack Santos has mentioned to me (in an e-mail of March 4, 2015) two genealogical works on the extended Wheelwright family through the generations: Steve J. Plummer, *The Wheelwright Genealogy* (n.p.: Cloth Wrap, 2010); and Plummer, *The Wheelwright Family Story* (n.p.: Cloth Wrap, 2010).

29. Michael P. Winship suggests that the conflict be termed the "free grace controversy"; see *Making Heretics: Militant Protestantism and Free Grace in Massachusetts, 1636–1641* (Princeton: Princeton University Press, 2002), 1.

30. For works about the Antinomian Controversy, see Donald D. Hall, ed., *The Antinomian Controversy, 1636–1638: A Documentary History*,

2nd ed. (Durham: Duke University Press, 1990); Winship, *Making Heretics*; and Eve LaPlante, *American Jezebel: The Uncommon Life of Anne Hutchinson, the Woman Who Defied the Puritans* (San Francisco: HarperSanFrancisco, 2003). See also my own works: *Threads*, "Poe and Hawthorne," and "Missing Man."

31. For William Hathorne's place as Salem deputy in the general court, see John A. Vinton, "The Antinomian Controversy of 1637," pt. 3, *Congregational Quarterly*, October 1873, 542–73 (see especially 558). For the earlier parts of this historical essay, see Vinton, "The Antinomian Controversy of 1637," pt. 1, *Congregational Quarterly*, April 1873, 263–85; pt. 2, *Congregational Quarterly*, July 1873, 395–426. Vinton corresponded with Ebenezer Wheelwright for a planned genealogy of the Wheelwright family, but it was never published. The correspondence, as well as the manuscript of "The Antinomian Controversy of 1637," is available at the New England Historical and Genealogical Society.

Introduction

1. These events included the false accusations of witchcraft in Salem, Massachusetts, and the resulting witchcraft trials and executions. *The Salem Belle* was published in the sesquicentennial of these events.

2. The phrase "popular delusions" suggests a possible source, Charles Mackay's *Memoirs of Extraordinary Popular Delusions*, 3 vols. (London: Richard Bentley, 1841). The date of the preface to Mackay's work is April 23, 1841; that of the J. N. L. letter in *The Salem Belle* is July 1841. The power of the irrational is a theme in both Mackay's study and Wheelrwright's novel. See also note 5 below.

3. *The Salem Belle* features language and events in the first half that correspond with language and events in the second half, thereby framing the center. An instance is the language here, "shipwreck" and "fatal rock," which recurs in chapter 14, page 153.

4. The phrase "perfect symmetry" is itself part of the novel's symmetry— see chapter 15, page 158.

5. Wheelwright's language in his introduction, "It is the object of the following pages . . . ," may have been drawn from the initial language in the preface to Mackay's *Memoirs of Extraordinary Delusions*, "The object of the Author in the following pages . . ." (1:v). Mackay does briefly

treat the Salem witchcraft delusion (see 2:305–9), drawing on Letter 8 of Sir Walter Scott's 1830 *Letters on Demonology and Witchcraft.*

Chapter First

1. This is Mount Auburn Cemetery, founded in Watertown and Cambridge in 1831.
2. Harvard College was founded in Cambridge, Massachusetts, in 1636.
3. Puritans were so named because they wished to purify the Church of England of its Catholic elements. They left England for the New World, especially from 1629 to 1640, in the Great Migration. Those settling in New England became part of the Massachusetts Bay Colony, founded in 1628.
4. "To catechize" is to teach children religious doctrine by requiring that they memorize the approved answers to a series of questions about the nature of that doctrine.
5. The phrase "true religion" is part of the symmetrical frame of the novel—see chapter 18, page 181.
6. General William Goffe (ca. 1605–ca. 1679) had authorized the execution of King Charles I (1600–49) in 1649 and supported Oliver Cromwell (1599–1658) during the Protectorate (1653–59), but upon the ascension of King Charles II (1630–85) to the British throne in 1660, Goffe escaped to New England, living in New Haven, Connecticut, and Hadley, Massachusetts. Nathaniel Hawthorne (1804–64) wrote a story about the legendary Goffe, titled "The Gray Champion" (1835).

Chapter Second

1. A "high churchman" was aligned with the Church of England and therefore opposed to the Puritans.
2. The James River is the chief waterway through Richmond, Virginia. It was named after King James I (1566–1625) of England (father of Charles I).
3. The *Sea Gull*, "under the command of Capt. Wing," is parallel to the later *Water Witch*, under the command of Captain Ringbolt (see page 158).
4. Slaves in the South were sometimes named after figures of classical history or mythology. Pompey was a great Roman general.

5. Pompey's view, anticipating by nearly a century the famous clause near the beginning of the Declaration of Independence, "that all men are created equal," led the reviewer for the *Pioneer*, probably editor James Russell Lowell (1819–91), to fault *The Salem Belle* for its anachronistic detail.

6. "Natural," or (as in the Declaration of Independence) "inalienable," rights are those intrinsic to man, not dependent on law.

7. The "black flag" is the pirate flag; the term is metaphorical here, for it is used to characterize a storm cloud.

8. In Roman mythology, Neptune was god of the sea.

9. The chain is akin to a lightning rod; it is a lightning conductor, intended to enable lightning to bypass a structure—here, a ship. This is another detail that the reviewer of *The Salem Belle* in the *Pioneer*, referring to Benjamin Franklin's later experiment with lightning, considered anachronistic.

10. The island near Boston Harbor where Roberts and Strale wandered later became just an outcropping of rocks.

11. The author sets Walter Strale's arrival in Boston on July 4, 1685, honoring in an extended passage the day of American independence, which would take place ninety-one years later. Ebenezer Wheelwright thereby introduces a historical tragedy, the Salem witchcraft frenzy, with a historical triumph.

12. At the time of this narrative, this building was the second Harvard Hall; it would burn down in 1764.

13. Wheelwright climaxes his patriotic passage with reference to the famous song (since 1931 the American national anthem), written by Francis Scott Key (1779–1843) in 1814 in response to the British bombardment during the Battle of Fort McHenry in Baltimore.

14. This was the motto of the Washington Light Infantry Company of Newburyport, Massachusetts, the town where Ebenezer Wheelwright grew up and to which he later returned.

Chapter Third

1. Originally Market Street and now State Street, King Street extended west from a major wharf into the city of Boston. In 1770 it was the site of the Boston Massacre.

2. A "drayman" is the driver of a cart for hauling goods.

3. The *Boston Post* (December 5, 1842) faulted the idea of "a *hotel* in the times of the Puritans." See appendix B, page 184.

4. Massachusetts lieutenant governor William Stoughton (1631–1701) was chief justice of the Court of Oyer and Terminer during the Salem witch trials. Samuel Sewall (1652–1730) served as a judge in that court, and he was the only judge who later apologized for his conduct. Samuel Willard (1640–1707), minister of the South Church, was a force for caution regarding the witchcraft accusations. And Waitstill Winthrop (1642–1717) was yet another judge in the Court of Oyer and Terminer during the witch trials.

5. Ezekiel Cheever (1614–1708) was the headmaster of Boston Latin School. His son Ezekiel Cheever (1655–1731) was the clerk at the Salem witch trials.

6. Boston in 1842 is compared to Troy in Homer's *The Iliad* (book 6).

7. This was Increase Mather (1639–1723), a minister in the North Church, who became president of Harvard College in 1692. Cotton Mather was his son.

8. This phrase is from Proverbs 13:12: "Hope deferred maketh the heart sick: but when the desire cometh, it is a tree of life" (King James Version).

Chapter Fourth

1. The phrase "the mountains of the moon" refers to the headwaters of the Nile River.

2. Samuel Willard, minister at the South Church, advocated restraint regarding the allegations of witchcraft in Salem; Cotton Mather (1663–1728), minister at the North Church (with his father, Increase Mather) advocated belief in spectral evidence and punishment of the accused.

3. According to the Old Testament book of Malachi, "But unto you that fear my name shall the Sun of righteousness arise with healing in his wings" (4:2, KJV). This image was taken by Christian readers as an anticipation of the coming of Christ in the New Testament.

4. The Puritans took natural events to constitute signs of divine will. This earthquake was considered a providential warning.

5. The "Rock of Ages," referring to Jesus, is also the title of a celebrated Christian hymn that first appeared in print in 1775, long after the action of *The Salem Belle*.

6. Cotton Mather quotes from Isaiah 26:20: "Come, my people, enter thou into thy chambers, and shut thy doors about thee: hide thyself as it were for a little moment, until the indignation be overpast" (KJV).

Chapter Fifth

1. Mary's brother, James Lyford, contends that Increase Mather will return from England with a new charter for the Massachusetts Bay Colony from King William III (1650–1702), whose armies had invaded England in 1688 ("Glorious Revolution") and prompted the flight of King James II (son of Charles II; 1603–1701). William was considered more sympathetic to Protestants than James, who had been sympathetic to Catholics. Increase Mather did indeed obtain the new charter.

2. With the naming of Mary Graham and the surprise that the identification prompts, Wheelwright offers the first element in another symmetrical pair that frames the center. For the second element in the pair, see page 125.

3. Roxbury was a town southwest of Boston that is now a neighborhood in Boston.

Chapter Sixth

1. These three towns are west of Boston—Worcester about 47 miles, Brookfield about 69 miles, and Hadley about 106 miles.

2. In 1660 King Charles II had sought the arrest of those responsible for the execution of his father, King Charles I, including the three who had escaped to New England: William Goffe, Edward Whalley (1607–75), and Timothy Dixwell (1607–89). The three men are honored in New Haven, Connecticut, by three streets: Goffe Street, Whalley Avenue, and Dixwell Avenue.

3. "The only Stuart who commands the sympathy and affection of posterity" was Charles I. Wheelwright is here expressing both admiration for and criticism of William Goffe.

4. According to Matthew 13:45–46, "that inestimable pearl" is "the kingdom of heaven," the "pearl of great price" (KJV).

5. The large public park in Boston ascends from Charles Street to the intersection of Beacon Street and Park Street, the location of the State House. At the time of the publication of *The Salem Belle*, Ebenezer

Wheelwright lived at 3 Temple Place, just off the Tremont Street side of the Boston Common.

6. By March 1692 Sarah Good and Sarah Osborne had been imprisoned in Salem.

7. These included the young girls' supposed fits and Tituba's testimony about her signing the devil's book.

8. This passage from "Mosaic scriptures" is Exodus 22:18 (KJV).

9. John Higginson (1616–1708) was not involved with the witchcraft trials.

10. Thomas Brattle (1657–1713) was a Boston merchant who criticized the Salem witchcraft proceedings. John Leverett (1662–1724), tutor at Harvard College, eventually became president of that institution. Mary Graham (Mary Lyford) is citing leaders who did not support the Salem witchcraft trials.

Chapter Seventh

1. This quatrain is the nineteenth in Thomas Gray's celebrated 1751 "Elegy Written in a Country Churchyard."

2. Wheelwright indicates his sense of his audience. Two extant copies of *The Salem Belle* are inscribed by mothers to daughters.

3. It is the hunger of James Lyford and Henry Temple upon finally reaching Worcester after eight days in a snowstorm that Isaac G. Reed refers to in his letter of January 26, 1843.

4. Such language suggests that Wheelwright may be honoring his devout father, Ebenezer Wheelwright Sr. (1764–1855).

Chapter Eighth

1. The idea was that one could go to the forest and sign the black book of the devil, thereby contracting to obey him. Hawthorne refers to this idea when he writes of the "Black Man" in *The Scarlet Letter*. See the conversations between Hester and Chillingworth (ch. 4, pp. 76–77), Hester and her daughter, Pearl (ch. 16, pp. 184–87), and Hester and Mistress Hibbins (ch. 22, pp. 241–42).

2. The "legends of Bagdad" probably refers to *The Thousand and One Nights* (or *The Arabian Nights*), and the "whole system of pagan fables" probably to the fables of Aesop and the Brothers Grimm.

3. Book 12 of Homer's *The Odyssey* recounts the alluring but dangerous sirens, listening to which could lead sailors to shipwreck.

Chapter Ninth

1. As the royal governor of Massachusetts in 1692, Sir William Phips (1651–95) convened the Court of Oyer and Terminer to address the witchcraft cases, and he advocated the ongoing prosecutions. By October 1692, however, he dissolved the court.

2. Robert Calef (1648–1719) was a strong opponent of the witch trials, publishing in London, in 1700, *More Wonders of the Invisible World*, responding to Cotton Mather's 1692 *Wonders of the Invisible World*.

3. The minister of the First Congregational Church of Boston was Joshua Moody (1633–97). The Third Congregational Church was Samuel Willard's South Church.

4. Cotton Mather's congregation was the Second Congregational Church, the North Church.

5. Here begins the extract from *The Salem Belle* that Ebenezer Wheelwright, as editor, included in the *Panoplist* (2, no. 11 [November 1868]: 336–44). With some trimming to the first paragraph, and otherwise only very slight revision, the extract continues on through the end of chapter 10. The work in the *Panoplist* is titled "A Sabbath in Boston in 1692" and begins with an introductory note that does not mention *The Salem Belle* or its author (335–36). The extracted section, titled "Extract from a Tale of 1692," comprising the opposing sermons of Samuel Willard and Cotton Mather, is the well-framed central section of the novel.

6. Romans 8:21 reads, "Because the creature itself also shall be delivered from the bondage of corruption into the glorious liberty of the children of God" (KJV).

7. The reference is to 2 Corinthians 5:1: "For we know that if our earthly house of this tabernacle were dissolved, we have a building of God, an house not made with hands, eternal in the heavens" (KJV).

8. Wheelwright is probably referring to *The Psalms, Hymns and Spiritual Songs of the Old and New Testament* (Boston, 1651), the third edition of *The Bay Psalm Book*.

9. The four stanzas are based on Psalms 51:1–3, 8–9.

10. These four stanzas are a blend of Lamentations 3:43–44 and 47–48 and Isaiah 26:20–21.

11. The source for this passage, 1 John 4:1, concludes, "because many false prophets are gone out into the world" (KJV).

12. According to 1 Kings 22:22, Micah, the prophet who truthfully tells Ahab that his venture is doomed, explains the incorrect favorable prophecies by stating that a spirit told God, "I will go forth, and I will be a lying spirit in the mouth of all his prophets" (KJV). Believing the lying prophets, Ahab enters the battle and is killed.

Chapter Tenth

1. Lyford's comment constitutes the center of the novel, offering in its contrast of light and dark the conflict illustrated between "true religion" and superstition.

2. This should be "xxviii:18," which reads, "And your covenant with death shall be disannulled, and your agreement with hell shall not stand; when the overflowing scourge shall pass through, then ye shall be trodden down by it" (KJV).

3. The full verse, 1 Peter 5:8, is, "Be sober, be vigilant; because your adversary the devil, as a roaring lion, walketh about, seeking whom he may devour" (KJV).

4. Mather is referring to the story of Saul, the first king of Israel, seeking guidance from the Witch of Endor; see 1 Samuel 28:3–25 (KJV).

5. Jesus overcomes evil spirits in Mark 1:21–39 (KJV).

6. Sternhold and Hopkins had been a standard book of psalms in England since the sixteenth century (1549).

Chapter Eleventh

1. The first victim was Bridget Bishop (1632–92), who was hanged on Gallows Hill.

2. Samuel Parris (1653–1720) delivered sermons that inflamed witchcraft fears. His daughter Elizabeth and his niece Abigail Williams were supposedly afflicted by fits, and his slave Tituba confessed to dealing with the devil, all helping lead to the witchcraft frenzy.

3. Parris alludes to Luke 9:62: "And Jesus said unto him, No man, having put his hand to the plough, and looking back, is fit for the kingdom of God" (KJV).

4. Trellison is referring to Genesis 22:1–18, wherein Abraham proves his fear of God by being willing to sacrifice his son Isaac.

5. Trellison is citing James 2:26: "For as the body without the spirit is dead, so faith without works is dead also" (KJV).

6. Rev. George Burroughs (1652–92) was accused of being a leader of the witches.

7. Mercy Lewis testified against George Burroughs with regard to his having brought her to the top of a mountain.

8. Wheelwright provides the second instance of the identification of Mary Graham and the surprised response, framing the center. For the first instance, see page 68.

9. Exodus 32:10 reads, in part, "Now therefore let me alone, that my wrath may wax hot against them" (KJV).

10. Jeremiah 2:34 reads, in part, "Also in thy skirts is found the blood of the souls of the poor innocents" (KJV).

11. This is an echo of the Lord's Prayer, Matthew 6:10: "Thy kingdom come. Thy will be done in earth, as it is in heaven" (KJV).

Chapter Twelfth

1. This was probably the farmer Joseph Putnam (1669–1725), an antagonist of Parris and an uncle of one of the accusing girls, Ann Putnam Jr.

2. Parris alludes to "the whole armour of God" (Ephesians 6:11–17), taking on which includes "above all, taking the shield of faith, wherewith ye shall be able to quench all the fiery darts of the wicked. And take the helmet of salvation, and the sword of the Spirit, which is the word of God" (6:16–17, KJV).

3. Having obtained the new charter for the Massachusetts Bay Colony, Increase Mather returned from England to Boston on May 14, 1692.

4. This was Bartholomew Gedney (1640–97), one of the judges of the Court of Oyer and Terminer in Salem.

5. This small park in Salem was a site for pasturing and for military drills. Off the Washington Square West side of the Salem Common is Mall Street: Nathaniel Hawthorne wrote *The Scarlet Letter* at 14 Mall Street.

6. These four lines, perhaps first encountered by Wheelwright in a hymn book, appear in William Cowper's (1731–1800) "Retirement" (1782), a tribute to bucolic contemplation.

7. The first session of the Court of Oyer and Terminer began on June 2, 1692; the second session would begin on June 28, 1692.

8. Mary alludes to Psalms 84:3: "Yea, the sparrow hath found an house, and the swallow a nest for herself, where she may lay her young, even thine altars, O Lord of hosts, my King, and my God" (KJV).

9. Hawthorne transformed elements of Wheelwright's account of the exchange between Mary Graham (Mary Lyford) and her brother, James Lyford (continuing through page 140), for chapter 17 of *The Scarlet Letter*, "The Pastor and His Parishioner."

10. Mary quotes a portion of 2 Corinthians 5:4: "For we that are in this tabernacle do groan, being burdened: not for that we would be unclothed, but clothed upon, that mortality might be swallowed up of life" (KJV).

Chapter Thirteen

1. About the same time—on July 19, 1692—five more accused witches were hanged: Sarah Good, Elizabeth How, Susannah Martin, Rebecca Nurse, and Sarah Wilds.

2. See 2 Corinthians 4:17: "For our light affliction, which is but for a moment, worketh for us a far more exceeding and eternal weight of glory" (KJV).

3. Governor Phips's wife was Mary Spencer Hull Phips. She was herself accused of witchcraft and was responsible for the release of one accused witch.

4. The governor found more repugnant than Mary's conviction for witchcraft her descent from regicide William Goffe.

5. The reviewers of *The Salem Belle* for the *New-York Evangelist* and the *Boston Recorder* objected to the strong criticism of Cotton Mather. See appendix B, pages 186 and 188.

6. George Burroughs was to be hanged with George Jacobs Sr., John Proctor, John Willard, and Martha Carrier.

Chapter Fourteen

1. Trellison echoes Jeremiah 20:14: "Cursed be the day wherein I was born" (KJV).

2. The "fatal hill" is Gallows Hill in Salem.

3. Nicholas Noyes (1647–1717) was a Salem minister who supported the witchcraft proceedings.

4. Sewall stood in the South Church as his confession was read by minister Samuel Willard.

5. This is the second instance of the language "shipwreck" and "fatal rock," here inverted; the first instance is on page 26. The symmetrical language frames the center.

6. Wheelwright quotes from Josiah Quincy III's *The History of Harvard University* (Cambridge, Mass.: Owen, 1840), 178.

7. The author relies on the language of Job 31:6—"Let me be weighed in an even balance that God may know mine integrity"—to refer to the Last Judgment.

Chapter Fifteenth

1. The *Water Witch* and Captain Ringbolt are parallel to the *Sea Gull* and Captain Wing (see page 36).

2. The phrase "perfect symmetry" is part of the symmetrical phrasing in *The Salem Belle*. For the earlier instance, see page 26.

3. Here begins the second passage in *The Salem Belle* that Hawthorne transformed, for chapter 20 of *The Scarlet Letter*, "The Minister in a Maze," and chapter 21, "The New England Holiday."

4. Bolton alludes to Romans 6:23: "For the wages of sin is death; but the gift of God is eternal life through Jesus Christ our Lord" (KJV).

5. Somers alludes to the Book of Esther, which concerns the persecution of the innocent. Haman, the king's minister, who was offended that Mordecai did not bow down to him, recommended to the king the destruction of the Jews. When Mordecai's cousin Queen Esther, who was Jewish, revealed this to her husband the king, he had Haman hanged on the gallows that Haman had intended for Mordecai. That gallows was "fifty cubits high" (Esther 5:14, 7:9).

6. In this context, Apollyon is Satan. Apollyon is mentioned in the New Testament in Revelation 9:11.

Chapter Sixteenth

1. The jailer, Harris, is afraid of the apparent figure of the devil and quotes Jesus, who was responding to Peter (Matthew 16:23 and Mark 8:33) and, more aptly here, to the devil (Luke 4:8).
2. This is the "manuscript" of "J. N. L." based on a lost "original chronicle" (see pages 25, 27).

Chapter Seventeenth

1. Harris alludes to the close of 2 Timothy 4:17: "I was delivered out of the mouth of the lion" (KJV).
2. Fire and brimstone are a punishment throughout the Bible, from Genesis, wherein Sodom and Gomorrah are destroyed with "brimstone and fire" (19:24, KJV) to Revelation, wherein the devil and his devotees are "cast alive into a lake of fire burning with brimstone" (19:20; see also 20:10 and 21:8, KJV).
3. Walter Strale taunts Harris and Bolton, quoting the first half of Proverbs 28:1 (KJV).
4. Here begins the third passage in *The Salem Belle* that Hawthorne transformed, for chapter 23 of *The Scarlet Letter*, "The Revelation of the Scarlet Letter," and chapter 24, "Conclusion."
5. Mary was saved from sacrifice to a false god. For biblical passages, see, for example, Leviticus 18:21 and 20:1–5 (KJV).
6. Trellison compares Gallows Hill to the "Mount of Offence," also known as the "mount of corruption" (II Kings 23:13), on Mount Olivet, the Mount of Olives.
7. Trellison alludes to Revelation 15–16 (KJV), in which the seven vials of the wrath of God are poured out.
8. Trellison refers to God speaking to Cain after the murder of Abel, in Genesis 4:10: "And he said, What hast thou done? the voice of thy brother's blood crieth unto me from the ground" (KJV).

Chapter Eighteenth

1. Trellison alludes to 1 Timothy 1:15, in which Paul states, "This is a faithful saying, and worthy of all acceptation, that Christ Jesus came into the world to save sinners; of whom I am chief" (KJV).

2. Wheelwright quotes with regard to the tree on Gallows Hill from the book he cites in his footnote, Abel Cushing's *Historical Letters on the First Charter in Massachusetts Government* (Boston: Bang, 1839), 162–63.

3. With the phrase "True Religion," Wheelwright completes another pair of framing symmetrical phrases; for the earlier instance of the phrase, see page 33.

DESIGNED AND TYPESET BY
Regina Starace

PRINTED AND BOUND BY
Sheridan Books

COMPOSED IN
Bodoni STD

PRINTED ON
Natures Natural

BOUND IN
Arrestox French Roast